Other novels by IMAFI

Family Affairs
Family Love Affairs

HOLD YOUR JUDGMENT

A NOVEL

IMAFI

iUniverse LLC
Bloomington

iUniverse books may be ordered through booksellers or by contacting:

iUniverse LLC
1663 Liberty Drive
Bloomington, IN 47403
www.iuniverse.com
1-800-Authors (1-800-288-4677)

Because of the dynamic nature of the Internet, any web addresses or
links contained in this book may have changed since publication and
may no longer be valid. The views expressed in this work are solely those
of the author and do not necessarily reflect the views of the publisher,
and the publisher hereby disclaims any responsibility for them.

Any people depicted in stock imagery provided by Thinkstock are models,
and such images are being used for illustrative purposes only.
Certain stock imagery © Thinkstock.

ISBN: 978-1-4759-9618-0 (sc)
ISBN: 978-1-4759-9620-3 (hc)
ISBN: 978-1-4759-9619-7 (e)

Library of Congress Control Number: 2013920937

Printed in the United States of America.

iUniverse rev. date: 11/23/2013

This novel is a work of fiction. Characters, names, events, and places are author's imagination. Any resemblance to actual persons, places, entities or events, other than actual public figures or celebrities used to make a point, is purely accidental.

DEDICATION

I dedicate this novel to my friends and clients, for their unconditional love and support. I simply want to say, from the bottom of my heart, thank you.

ACKNOWLEDGEMENTS

I want to thank my focus group for their priceless suggestions and recommendations. I particularly want to thank the individuals that edited the manuscript with perseverance, agony, and tolerance, because of the novel's adult contents and/or vulgarity—they are morally closer to God's representatives on earth. I agreed. I'm also grateful for their prayers, on my behalf, to their good Lord, to cleanse my soul. However, I do have one more request from these perfect outstanding citizens. Y'all must continue to pray for me because I have many souls. I've used three souls, to-date.

CHAPTER 1

Assistant Bishop, Mrs. Florence Shackles, sat in her opulent den at the end of her busy day. She had just completed her missionary assignments as the committee chair of the community empowerment program of the Holy Saints Fifth Mount Olive Baptist Church. Her lifelong project to reduce teenagers' high school dropouts always left her exhausted by the end of each missionary assignment. She admitted, in private, to close friends, that her fight to achieve her dream was an uphill battle that would take another generation.

This day, however, she wanted a few seconds before she called her husband, Bishop Shackles, to see how his day went at the Baptist convention in Memphis. He had been summoned to appear before its governing board to explain his recent Easter Sunday sermons in which he embraced all children of God: men, women, old, young, gays, lesbians, and non-believers, into his ministry.

In another week, she would be hosting the annual deaconess board retreat where she intended to step down as the chair. She had just been appointed as the secretary general of the Progressive United African Baptist Church Women Congress, headquartered, on the island of Madagascar, off the eastern coast of Africa.

With a cup of green tea, a dash of Ghanaian herbs, and Al Green's *let's stay together;* playing at the background,

1

she opened the special golden anniversary edition of her sorority's magazine, *XXX Bunny, Soro News.*

The only feature in the magazine was an exposé of two of the sorority's eminent emeriti, Sheila Samson (a.k.a, Forklift) and attorney Patricia Peterman (a.k.a, DeeClare). The piece was written by the magazine's editor in chief, W. Jones (a.k.a, DIP), a past President of the same outfit.

Mrs. Shackle immediately changed her choice of refreshments of herb tea and honey to a glass of white wine. She knew the two soror sisters first hand. They were classmates in college. In fact, one of them was the godmother of her daughter, Samoa.

If memory of the two eminent ladies served her right, she knew it would be a juicy reading. As fate would have it, her children had gone to bed for the night. She didn't want any interruptions.

She adjusted her seat and started reading:

Hold Thy Judgment: Two of Our Own Tell All
By
W. Jones, editor in chief, *XXX Bunny Soro News.*

Deeclare (Pat), opened the latest e-mail from Forklift (Sheila), on her made in USA 15-inch, pink laptop while she snuggled with her husband, Paul, skin to skin, in their Egyptian custom-made orthopedic bed with dual temperature controls. It was a cold night. Her husband was in a romantic mood and wanted to make love. She just wanted to cuddle, instead.

Pat smiled as she read Sheila's e-mail. Sheila's e-mails had been more frequent, erotic, and more sexually explicit lately.

"Is that Sheila again? Paul asked. Tell her to leave my wife alone and get a life. If I didn't know you, I would've thought you want her more than me."

"Stop it Paul and go back to sleep," she replied.

As she was responding to Forklift's e-mails under the cover, her husband was fingering her pussy to wetness with one hand, palming her razor sharp nipples with the other, and at the same time reading over her shoulder. All Pat wanted to do was concentrate on Sheila's e-mail. She removed Paul's hand from her pussy and said, "Please, stop it. I want to finish reading her e-mails."

As with most nights, Paul rolled over and pretended to be sleeping. Making love to his wife every fortnight was becoming a routine and frustrating, at best. His marriage, for sometimes now, has been on a slippery slope into a sexless and passionless love affair.

In their last e-mail exchanges, Sheila agreed to a brunch with Pat on Sunday after Pat's church service, at a secluded café on the Boulevard to further discuss in details the contents of their e-mails. Their feelings for each other were almost mutual, except there was one problem . . .

Even though Sheila was equally nervous, she showed up early for the brunch just to watch Pat in her famous red stiletto as she sailed towards her like a diva. They smiled at each other and hugged gently. To a detached onlooker, their meeting would be construed as two innocent professional women out for brunch on a typical Sunday, after church service. Sheila ordered a glass of white wine for herself and a virgin strawberry daiquiri for Pat. She knew Pat so well. She had done her homework . . .

They sat at the far corner of the café. Within minutes, their knees touched slightly underneath the table for the first time. Pat looked around the room full of church goers from different denominations to see if everyone was watching with suspicion and disgust. At one point, Pat felt she was having brunch with a foreign double agent. Far from it, she was just suffering from premature quilt, even though she hadn't done anything out of the ordinary. Sheila was equally nervous; to say the least, she just didn't give a damn who may be watching.

They looked directly into each other's eyes like new lovers. There was definitely a love gesture from one of parties sitting at the table. At last, after five years of living in the same community, there was almost a meeting of the minds . . . of sexual intentions, at least.

Sheila cleared her throat and said, "Pat, your e-mails, even though detached, touched my heart. I mean that. I couldn't believe why it took me so long to express my interest in you after thcse many years we've known each other. Maybe I should've said something since I first felt you, but I was a little nervous. Honestly, I never knew if I would seem pushy. I was also scared of your rejection. Trust me, Pat, I've dreamed of you many times. Many nights, I wanted to call just to hear your beautiful voice. I had been curious how it would feel to see you close and personal . . ."

Pat interrupted her and said, "Thanks for your interest and compliments but there is one problem: I'm not into females at all. It's not one of my fantasies either. I've never thought of being with a woman. I love and prefer dick so much . . . You can even say, I'm strictly dickly."

Sheila smiled and sipped a little wine . . .

Pat then continued:

"However, you may be shocked to know that my husband and I spoke of you a lot lately as well. On a few occasions (can I be honest, Shelia?), we discussed if it would be possible to have you just for him on our fifteenth year wedding anniversary. All I want out of it is to watch. Some call it voyeurism, I believe. I love watching . . . we did it once at Kill Devil Hills . . . Don't get me wrong, we are not into open marriage but I had decided a long time ago that I'll do all within my power to keep my marriage alive, interesting, and lasting. I wanted it just for him. Frankly, I've been neglecting him lately. Think about it Sheila, you will not be disappointed, if you agree with my proposition. I know what you may be thinking at this moment, but that's all I can offer you at this time. I beg your pardon, that's all I can offer you, period. By the way, you look gorgeous and smelled damn good at our last soro meeting."

"I never knew you noticed," Sheila replied,

I think your Ted (D.R) is over compensated." Pat responded.

Sheila smiled and said. "What does 'D.R' stand for?"

"Never mind," Pat replied.

———————————————•●•———————————————

Sheila's cell rang. It was her husband calling to tell her he would be coming home late.

"Who might that be? I hope you're not in trouble?" Pat asked.

"That was Ted working late tonight as usual. He doesn't know I'm here with you. By the way, he can't stand your ass."

"The feeling is mutual," Pat replied.

They both laughed.

"Pat, what you're asking me isn't what I've in mind but I'll think about it if only to please you," Sheila said, as she was placing her right hand on Pat's lap and started to massage it gently.

For a moment, Pat seemed to enjoy it. Or maybe, she was being polite and/or scared. Moments later, she pulled away her chair to discourage any temptations.

"This is crazy and isn't right," Pat told herself.

"Do you mind Pat, if I invite you to my home this afternoon, to keep me company for few minutes? At least, let me fix you late lunch with a glass of my vintage wine to celebrate this first meeting. I really don't want to be alone this afternoon."

Pat smiled, glowed, and accepted Sheila's invitation like a teenager on her first approved formal date by her active military sergeant's father.

On Sheila's insistence, Pat left her 550E 2012 Mercedes Benz SUV at an apartment complex's parking lot, across from a shopping mall, opposite the restaurant, and rode home with her. It was only a fifteen-minute drive.

After parking her car, Sheila invited Pat into her home. She immediately offered her a chilled glass of sweet white wine. It seemed she had envisioned how the day would progress. So far, she was 100 percent on target. What a genius.

Sheila's house was gorgeous. Although not as big as Pat's, it was perfect for a thirty-something year old certified public accountant of a major federal government contractor, headquartered in Zandria, Virginia. She is married to Theodore (Ted) Samson, a retired marine officer, and currently a part-time single-family real estate developer of low to middle—income families.

They lived comfortably as a suburbia middle class with a swimming pool and a four-car garage. They have one puddle. No cat. Ted's son is allergic to cats. Their perfectly manicured lawn, under annual maintenance contract with an African American owned landscaping company, and all Mexican work-force, was the talk of the neighborhood, among other matters of interest.

With combined salary and retirement income over six figures, her family enjoyed the best life could offer. They had an annual one-month vacation by design: two weeks overseas and two weeks in the continental United States.

Sheila excused herself. As she was walking towards the kitchen, she started taking off her jacket to reveal her tight spaghetti—strap silk blouse showing her bare shoulders with her large hard nipples gently moving below her thin silk camisole as she walked. She planned to be braless for the occasion. Her body tone and physique made it unnecessary. She never liked to wear a bra unless it was absolutely necessary. One of those necessary occasions was when attending PTA meetings. She was the chair of the PTA finance committee of her son's former grade school. Her little project, in the powerful helicopter mother-dominated organization, was teaching basic ABC of finance to second grade students. She believed it was never too early to teach kids about the power and management of the American dollar. "Save and invest early," was her motto.

7

Mother Teresa would be proud of her attire at all PTA events.

For a 38-year old woman, Sheila was like a goddess of the sea and a dream to anyone who knew her and wanted her. Yes, many wanted her. She was perfect in every way imaginable. Her skin was smooth. Her body tone was like a model on the cover of the Mademoiselle magazine, except that her picturesque beauty was original and untouched by photo shop.

Her breasts were soft, robust, full, and would've been perfect for a "cleavage" competition, if there was ever one. Her bosom was rumored to be 40C, in reality, it was only 34DD. She just knew how to wear her push-up bra brilliantly. Her walk was intoxicating and mesmerizing. She had it all . . . , and at a distance, her chest could be compared to an African American female day-time-celebrity talk show host on television.

Her choreographed sultry demeanor gave Pat a glimpse of what she was being offered on a silver platter with zero calories. Many remotely close to her had salivated over her cleavage and overall beauty. For a mother of two, God had been good to her in every way possible. Frankly, the good Lord had been great to her. She was definitely created on God's day of rest.

"Sitting in my living room is a gorgeous woman I want to have but pretending not to notice me," Sheila said to herself about Pat. Of course, she was wrong. Pat was watching and her erotic zones were also paying attention, even though she wasn't into women.

As Sheila went into her kitchen, she quickly reminded herself and said, "Sheila, you must control yourself. In a matter of time; she'll be my play doll."

"Sheila, whatever you're cooking smells good. I'm starving," Pat said softly from the living room.

Sheila smiled and shouted from the kitchen, "Pat, can I refresh your glass, dear?"

"Yes, but that will be my limit. You know I've got to drive later, unless you want to carry me home."

"My pleasure dear, my pleasure indeed," Sheila said aside.

"Slip of the tongue but I wouldn't mind to oblige her," Sheila murmured to herself as she poured the wine.

"Are you saying something, Sheila?" Pat asked.

"Nothing dear," Sheila replied.

Thirty minutes or so later, with her hand under a spoon full of her secret hot and spicy Louisiana sauce; she brought Pat a taste of her cooking. Carelessly, she mistakenly blew over the sauce into Pat's designer white-silk-tight tank top. She probably did it intentionally . . . smooth operator . . .

"My goodness, I'm sorry Pat. I didn't mean to do that. I hope I've not ruined your beautiful top? I may have to buy you another one," she exclaimed.

"That's ok, Sheila," Pat said, as she stood and went to the bathroom to remove the stains from her blouse. Minutes later, she returned to the living room and nervously covered her chest with a towel with one hand and used the other hand to hold the damped blouse.

Sheila took the blouse and spread it on her bed post to air out. She then gently placed the spoon full of sauce on Pat's mouth.

Sultrily, she slurped the remaining sauce in the spoon, after her, the same way two lovers would at the blooming stage of a dream love affair.

When lunch was ready, Sheila brought Pat a plate of medium rare marinated boneless, lightly breaded lamb, imbedded in sautéed organic brown baby mushrooms, red onions, oregano, hot curry, and red pepper, that had baked slowly with light butter in a 200-degree oven for two hours and thirty minutes. Normally, the delicacies should have been baked for one hour fifteen minutes at 450 degrees.

Sheila knew the slower the baking process, the more time she could spend with her potential soon to be lover. She wanted to enjoy every minute of their first union together.

Sheila ought to write a screen play for the folk in Hollywood on "How to seduce a doubtful potential lover in two hours on a first date and scored."

After all, she had not cooked for her own husband since their son left for college over four months ago. If truth be told, she would have preferred to have Pat's milk and cookie for lunch instead of the elaborate lunch. That reality would have to wait.

During and after lunch, they spoke about their graduate school and sorority days.

They laughed, as they remembered their sorority's social secretary, Ann Mary, who became a sex therapist just to satisfy her sexual dreams, and at the same time, render much needed specialized services to clients searching to enhance and/or improve their marriages and sex lives.

Ann Mary also wanted to make a ton of money with her sexual desires and endeavors. She did make a lot of money. God bless her.

CHAPTER 2

Ann Mary had her college degree in Sociology, a master's degree in Public Health Administration, and a PhD in psychology of sexual freedom and democracy. She was gorgeous with a big sexual appetite. Like in the movie *Basic Instinct*, she was built like Roxie, walked like Roxie, jealous like Roxie, and teased like Roxie. However, she was different from Roxie in two ways: She had bigger boobs than Roxie, and she never ran her car over an embankment and killed herself in a jealous rage like Roxie.

She loves to wear everything tight and fitted. Everything about her was tight. Her shoulder length hair extensions were tight. Her breasts were succulent, soft, but tight—she never breast fed her children. Her belly was tight. Her thighs were tight. Even, after three children, her pussy was rumored to be tight. The tightness of her pussy couldn't be verified objectively from those who confessed to have sampled it or many that lied they did. The rumors about her tight pussy were plastered all over Facebook and Twitter, nonetheless. The only soft but firm part of her body was her soft-jelly-like bouncing butt, her killer badonkadonk.

Her sexual consulting firm, Ann Mary 4 Yu, LLC, (AM4U) was incorporated in the state of Delaware, with operations in OldPort. It was a thriving gender neutral establishment catered only to married couples. The basic requirement was simple—couples must be happily married to some extent, and one hundred percent in agreement with the therapy. The therapy wasn't to cure but to improve sexual relationships.

She only scheduled one couple/client a day, Monday through Friday, except in the summer months which were reserved for couples from oil producing states in the country and abroad.

Two weekends a month were set aside for office meetings with her professionally trained staff for strategic planning sessions.

She was once offered a vintage hand-crafted original 1948 Bentley just for one Saturday session in December, to coach a newlywed Prince, married to a fifteen year-old virgin in a prearranged marriage. She declined. As she later confessed to one of her regular office fuck-mates, she wanted no part of a corrupt royal family fucking every underage citizen in their Kingdom. She had ethical standards and morals. She was not for sale that way. Not at their offering price, anyway.

Her office was spacious, built on the beach with seventy percent of the glass windows overlooking the Atlantic Ocean.

Her female clients loved her services because she had saved their marriages with substantial new and improved sexual innovations. To-date, she had a 90 percent approval rate from that market sector.

Her male clients adored her beauty and agility. She showed them how to enjoy sex as well as pleasure their wives to unforgettable orgasm within fifteen minutes or less, guaranteed.

From the male clients, she had 98 percent satisfaction rate. The remaining two percent despised her just for the heck of it because they wanted to stay with their wives and also fuck her exclusively, at her price.

She turned down many of her male clients' advances. She was very selective of whom she went to bed with. She only violated her rules under her own terms. After all, it was against her professional code of ethics, "Thou shall not fuck thy clients if not required by therapy." Another one of her self-monitored contract loopholes . . .

Her contract agreement, summarized below, was drafted by the consortium of Ivy League law professors and one semi-retired stripper, was very specific and air tight. Two of the original drafters of the contract were her former satisfied clients.

No sex therapy outside office consultation.

Couple must be present at all therapy sessions.

Couple must be tested for all sorts of diseases. Copies of all medical records must be sent to her office 30 days before therapy—safe sex is a priority because many lives are at risk, under her hegemony.

Clients weren't allowed to take any sex enhancement performance drugs 30 days before therapy.

Couple must have had sex the last six hours before therapy.

Appointments had to be scheduled thirty-three days in advance (she was 33 years old when she opened for business)

Office staff is exclusively male, under 30, and without any political and religious affiliations.

All notes taken during therapy must be shredded at the end of therapy engagement contract (she had a big business with the "Shred it" local franchise so much so she had a forty percent volume discount. She once earned a 7-day, all fees paid vacation to Disneyland, Europe.)

Basic fees range from $12,599.56 to 49,999.56 with a required $10,000.56 nonrefundable security deposit. The remaining balance must be paid by the beginning of initial therapy session. Potential clients are advised to call for current rates within thirty days of therapy or go online for the latest information on anything from up-to-date contract updates, alumni club membership applications or completing the referral/client page for a chance to win a 14-day cruise for two in Paris, Casablanca, or Bagdad. Jamaica and Costa Rica are slated to be added in the future.

A not-to-sue waiver, for any reasons, must be signed before any therapy services.

She had two levels of services—gold and deluxe. Both services included full use of limousine services, formal dining, dance lessons, movies (options—romance, aggressive-dominant, porn, light-dominant), massages, shower scenes, Jacuzzi sessions, and the so called, happy-happy sexual combo.

Facility privileges included a commercial gourmet kitchen supervised by a world renowned chef and a kitchen staff of eleven. The food menu comprised of domestic and international cuisines. Special diet menus were available. The wine cellar was internationally designed and stocked. The average price of any vintage wine was $345. Alcohol, although not recommended, was available free of charge—she had her undisclosed reasons for such freebies . . .

Clients had access to her ten thousand sq. ft. opulent consulting empire. It was large enough to accommodate a movie theater, a dance studio, five bathrooms, a commercial gourmet kitchen, eight bedrooms, four massage rooms, two formal dining rooms, an art gallery, and a boutique owned and managed by a well-known New York 5th avenue fashion outfit. Five star hotels can't even come close in this part of the hemisphere.

Employees are sworn to confidentiality and bonded to the tune of $3 million dollars for life, all paid by her firm, MA4U, LLC.

Couple can't have more than two therapy sessions during marriage.

Ten percent discount for the second therapy.

No video or audio taping of therapy sessions.

Her corporate jet was available for lease with forty percent discount to deluxe card carrying members.

She does not fuck women.

Written in bold red letters across the middle of the fifteen page contract were:

Couple must perfect their 69 sexual positioning by the end of therapy.

Condoms must be used during intimate sex therapy if she participated in happy-happy.

Clearly written across each page of the contract were the following words in bold red capital letters: *RESULTS ARE NOT GUARANTEED WITHOUT YOUR GUARANTEE.*

Recently, she has been reviewing the possibility of expanding her services to include engaged couples with specific marriage date. To her, a love boot camp is the key to a lasting relationship. What a genius!

Her sex therapy was custom-made for each couple/client.

Her soon to-be-published book on Kindle only version, "Do Me Right," about how to achieve a balanced and fulfilled marriages in modern day America is summarized below:

Determine, on your first date, if sex only is the goal or life companionship is the objective.

Stay away from alcohol and drugs during the developmental stage of your relationship—you need a clear head for a good decision.

Stop blaming your partner for sexual or any other disappointments in your life.

Evaluate yourself to ascertain if you are ready for a meaningful relationship. Everyone else can't be wrong all the time.

Study and answer the relationship questionnaires in the novel, *Family Love Affairs by imafi* before engaging in any serious relationship.

Don't be a desperate love seeker. Patience is golden, unless you have reason or reasons to do otherwise.

Ask your partner about your behavior, habits, or characters he or she doesn't like during the first month of dating to recognize each other's likes and dislikes before any commitment and/or sex.

Use indirect ways to find out what your partner does or doesn't like—if he or she says, "I don't like that dress or that chic wears too much makeup or my friend is a lazy bump or my sister is a bitch, or your friend has a cool butt, or my mother is a great cook," these are signals for you to look at yourself, and see if you have the same attributes. The comments may be about you. It's like a parable, analyze each comment . . .

Respect your partner at all times and never take each other for granted.

Be real for real.

Don't impose your values or ways of doing things on your partner. Remember, you were raised differently, probably from different cultures, race, backgrounds, and life experiences.

Don't bring all your baggage and drama into a relationship. Sooner or later, it would affect communications and ruin the relationship before you know it. Otherwise, seek someone like you, with similar baggage and drama. Good luck in your endeavor.

Remember that it's not easy for a squire peg to fit a round hole, as such, don't expect your partner to accept you as you are, or see things your way. You can't change anyone. If you're delusional to think you can, it would be temporary, at best. Don't take my words for it, read all about it in the library.

Remember, love doesn't operate in a vacuum. So, prevent problems before you vow to resolve them. A word of wisdom—a damaged car will never be the same, even after it has been repaired.

Appreciate each other. Cultivate good manners with and for each other. Learn to say *thank you* for simple things. Remember, no one owns anyone anything in life. Learn to enhance the good aspects of one another, find amicable ways to correct any deficiencies, and move on . . .

Stop postponing your sexual enjoyment until your children turn eighteen or leave home—in today's modern family, they may never leave home.

Don't substitute your children or other living souls in your household with your relationship—find a way to simultaneously manage and balance every aspect of your life. Yes, learn to multi-task . . .

Remember, one man's meat is another man's poison. Therefore, choose your own poison wisely. Once you do, stop bitching about it.

Improve your own life during your relationship.
Set individual goals and achieve them together, if
possible. Earn your respect. Earn your independence.

Don't be too smart for your own good. Treat your
partner with admiration. If you do otherwise, your
pomposity will catch up with you sooner than later,
and with regrets—stop pretending. Love isn't a game
of monopoly.

Don't manage love by your own definitions.
Remember that your partner has his or her own
definitions too. At times, love definitions may not be
mutually inclusive.

Place your bedroom as far away as possible from
children's bedrooms, guestrooms, and the den. If need
be, sound proof your bedroom. The renovation cost is
worth it.

Bedroom doors should have a latch or deadbolt. Use it.

Avoid unsolicited disturbances during love making,
unless such disturbance is part of the act, the house is
on fire, or a lasting Middle East peace is about to be
declared. The latter may even be a joke. Concentrate
on the good stuff . . .

Give your partner what he or she wants instead of
rationalizing the moral justifications to the contrary.
Sexual morality is subjective and indeed ok. Be ready
and willing to give your partner what he or she can't
obtain anywhere else—respect, love, fantastic sex,
understanding, caring; peace of mind, support, and
appreciation.

Remember, your partner is not your mother, father, child, or any other relatives. Keep in mind that you are in a two-person partnership, first and foremost.

Don't ignore or improperly manage your marriage or relationship. If you do, your relationship and the benefits thereof will surely evaporate sooner than expected. Read my book: *Optimizing marriage Partnerships.*

Know your sex partner. Learn what turns each other on or off. Pleasing your partner, in any form, must be a top priority. A relationship is not a TV reality show like those housewives of somewhere . . . That's all the more reason nearly all their relationships never last. Google it . . .

Don't force or impose your annoying habits on your partner—accept me the way I'm, may be ok, provided you are willing and ready to accept your partner's ways and habits as well. Better yet, seek only a partner that will accept you for who you are (at a price, of course), otherwise, such ideology is unrealistic, asinine, delusional, and frankly, stupid, to say the least.

Remember, anything and everything you do will affect your relationship, especially your sex connections. For example, find out if your partner doesn't mind you snorting or bringing your beloved pet to bed, or watching *Days of our lives* during foreplay and/or sex. Otherwise, don't do these things.

Don't assume anything in a relationship. If you want to do things your way, that's fine, dandy, encouraged, but remain the fuck alone, in your little world. To this end, I can only wish you God's speed for your narrow mind. By the way, that's not a prayer; I'm just laughing out loud (LOL) after you fucked-up, and then blame someone else, as usual.

If your partner snores, likes to watch TV in bed, hugs the bed sheet, or reads in bed with the lights on, please, sleep in separate rooms to keep the peace. If you are untidy and love to leave your shit all over the bathroom, please, have his and her bathrooms. If old habits die hard, please die with your old habits alone. It's your right to do so. Learn to be happy with yourself without expecting anyone to understand. Don't drag anyone else into your tentacles of unhappiness and misery.

Recognize the facts of life and adjust to the circumstances of the day—don't accommodate your disrespectful children, your arrogant brother-in-law, your overbearing mother in-law, your inconsiderate friends, and your military styled father, as additions and/or part of your relationship. Be mindful of your reactions to your partner by avoiding irritating behavior. Minimize endless discussions on everything under the sun, all of the time—constant nagging, untidiness; who is fucking who in Hollywood, the price of oil, which cola product tastes better, what Pastor Sunshine said at the pulpit last Sunday, and what her Royal Highness, Oprah Winfrey, said last week about climate change. Stop the endlessly speech about your friend's recent separation, divorce or whatever else they are doing. Your partner may not want to hear about the slut in your office sleeping with your boss, who is also fucking the boss's nineteen-year old stepson working at the mailroom. Your partner may not want a book report on your relatives that died fifty years ago, or your constant bitching because you have a bad hair day, or you are too fat, too short, or too thin, and so on and so forth. Each behavior will sabotage your sexual connections. Instead, talk about each other with love and affection. Got my drift now?

Create valuable time with your partner and make it memorable, instead of injecting poison-pill behavior. As the saying goes, "When you are in Rome, do what the Romans do." That simply means: respect and pay attention to the values cherished by each other when you are together. Don't be a princess or a prince when you are not from a royal family. Got it?

At a minimum, plan sex once a week, or at least be romantic once a week—by all means necessary, make it happen. Don't assimilate blindly the rules of others. Stay real in your sexual expectations. Don't plan sex only on special events: anniversary, birthday, etc. After all, you don't have to eat turkey only on Thanksgiving . . . Be creative, flexible, adventurous, and adaptable. Make sex fun, challenging, and enjoyable—find time for it. Like any successful endeavors, you must work hard at your relationship to be successful at it, if you want it. Life is too short, live like it, and stop talking about it. By now, you ought to know that the grass is no longer greener at the other side of the fence.

The idea that men over 40 have less sex, according to the gospel of music super star, Miley Cyrus, is idiotic, at a minimum. There is no direct correlation between age and sex. Many factors may contribute to less sex between partners, at any age, including but not limited to: length of relationship, stress (natural, manufactured or self-imposed), finances, degree of expectations, undue outside influences, health issues, behavior, children, pets, lack of excitement in the relationship . . . . and you name it. All humans under the age of thirty-something, are less likely to be preoccupied with such sex killing or worldly issues. As a result, they have more time for love and sex. In fact, young people probably talk and think mostly about sex and not about mortgage payments or what's for dinner—may God bless their innocent souls. Amen.

Selfishness is not a good ingredient for a lasting relationship. Learn to share. Learn to appreciate. Learn to give. Don't take for granted any support or understanding you receive from your partner, no matter how small they may be. It's always a blessing to be cared for in any way or fashion. Love or caring is not an inalienable right. Cherish and adore it when you found one. It's getting harder to find the so-called good men or women, in the market nowadays. Let me ask you, how long have you been shopping around for Mr. or Ms. Right? I rest my case . . .

If you must, listen to yourself. If you have to, listen to your partner and then create your own togetherness. Create an atmosphere conducive to sexual exuberance. Stay away from rigid "How to enjoy sex rules" as seen on TV sex therapy programs or from self-acclaimed sex gurus. Sometimes, the best sex rule is, "No sex rules." Grow up and think . . .

By the way, discuss with or let your partner how you prefer your sex cooked—light, medium light, well light, nasty, nasty light, medium nasty, extreme nasty, Chef's special, or combination thereof. In other words, express yourself about the sex acts you desire. Don't wait for your partner to lead you to the kingdom of heaven, all the time, unless it was designed and agreed to as such. Think about it, my friends.

Act as if you're still single each day you are with your mate—single but married, if that's how far along you are in your relationship. Marriage doesn't and shouldn't diminish or eliminate your individuality or affect what you are made of. However, be yourself only when acceptable by your partner. Listen to each other's needs, fantasies, and then take a pleasurable ride of your life. Otherwise, stop bitching, stay single, and be miserable or be happy, if that's how you had convinced yourself, to-date.

Remember, no one is an island. If you want to be an island, stay far away from the shore where no one can easily get to you. Yes, you can stand your ground and do things your way, only if you could afford to do so—not like the Florida gun law about the phrase. Even that law hasn't had happy ending for all concern, to-date. Be realistic and accept the consequences of your resolve—you can't plant grapes and expect to harvest oranges, at least, not in a foreseeable future. If it happens, it wouldn't taste like the original organic specimen.

Be ready and willing to change. At a minimum, adjust whatever you are and/or believed in, under the circumstances. Accept the fact that no two individuals are created the same, even twins. After all, we do change or adjust for grand-mama, employer, doctor, the law, teacher, preacher, and so forth, in order to get what we want, especially when we are in need . . . If you find what is good for you and you want to keep it, you must be ready to accommodate and bend over backward. Translation: change or adjust. The talk about one cannot change is bullshit, not if you want to keep what you like. If you don't, there are plenty of people without the "Me too mentality" waiting for you to fuck up and rush to take your place—read all about the surveys and statistics on the World Wide Web.

Associate yourself with a smart partner who may be going places. Someone with knowledge, someone who can obtain knowledge, someone with open mind, someone who is willing to learn, someone with intellectual curiosity, and someone anxious to improve him or herself—not necessarily someone with college degrees, any idiot can obtain one of those these days. Correction: there are many folks with college degrees and much more, in the history of the world, who never add value to their lives or the lives of others. Are you one of those? Just checking . . .

Seek someone you can look up to. Someone who can make your life better, more challenging, more productive, and more fulfilling—the Clintons and the Obamas are two famous current examples. Otherwise, accept your choice and stop bitching to everybody about it. As Judge Judy Sheindlin will say, "You pick him." If you pick your so-called looser, it's your entire fault—obviously, you are not all that smart to begin with. Stop blaming your partner for an association you are a willing participant. It takes two . . .

Be patient and seek your own type, for a meaningful relationship or love, the same way water finds its own level. Opposite hardly attracts—if it does, by coincidence, it wouldn't last. For example, if you like to smoke or whatever, look for someone that smokes, or whatever. If you like pets, look for someone who likes pets. If you nag and love to misbehave like the paid-to-act brides on the Bridezilla TV show, look for someone who will accommodate your nuances. You can only impose your values on others to a limited extent. For heaven's sake, reality shows are only entertainment and only that, entertainment.

Accommodate your partner only if you want to and not because you have to. Don't compromise. Why would you compromise on a lousy food in a restaurant or a poor service from you Doctor or lawyers, or even from your government? If you do, it will always leave a sour taste in your mouth. Pay attention to each other even in trivia things. Many times, petty things can wreck a promising relationship. Remember, little things add up to big things, especially if such little things are unchecked early. Like any disease, prevention is better than cure. As the saying does, "Little drops of water make the mighty ocean."

Don't substitute or accommodate your children, pets, family members, or friends in your relationship—yes, including your favorite son, daughter, or Poodle, who always comes first in your life. You and your partner must come first at all times. As the good Book says, "Seek ye first the kingdom of God and all other things will be added unto thee." Take care of each other first and all other things will follow. Remember, one day, your favorite darlings will leave your ass, moved on, and you will have little or nothing to show for the lost love or relationship with your partner. I stand corrected; you can always get another pet, if you don't have any already, to continue the charade . . . Take inventory of your life and see what's missing.

Learn all the dos and don'ts of your partner and make them part of your daily routine. In the end, believe in yourself and your partner and not as much on the advice of experts or the so called genius on love or sexual matters. These folk won't live with you. Objectively, learn to recognize your shortcomings, your partner's shortcomings, and work hard to minimize the gap. Keep in mind one fact—parents don't teach their children how to manage love or relationships outside mother-father-child circle. Therefore, the ideas you grew up with or the ideas you thought were great in your head, as a single unattached individual, and/or those propagated by mommy dearest and father goose, maybe a mirage and unfit for relationships beyond your family and gang of friends. What's the solution? Simply rebrand yourself at any age, based on the facts and circumstances surrounding your current love objectives. Otherwise, you will join the fifty-five percent of divorcees and eighty percent of relationships that went south in three years or less.

Don't walk in other people's shoes to design or redesign your relationship. Don't equate other folk's sex life with yours. Remember, two feet of the same size may not necessarily fit the same shoe. For example, if your partner snores, don't start to kick or nag him or her as everyone seems to suggest. Instead, go to another room or sleep on the couch until you can find solutions to the problem. Another example, don't force each other to watch the same TV programs—remember, you were individuals before your so-called, sweet togetherness. The most understanding and accommodation you will ever get in your life time is from your mommy and daddy that spoiled your ass, and a few family members who had pretended throughout your life, how much they love you. Individuals have needs, space, and solitude—you have no virtue on needs. One more thing, people will talk behind your back—the question is; are you listening, and if you are listening, are you making necessary adjustments?

Let peace of mind reign in your household, period. Let your house be a peaceful castle. Spend quality time together and don't take each other for granted—at the end of the day, hug and kiss before you rant about what the politicians are up to, send each other love notes, cards, and relax with a glass or glasses of vintage wine. If you don't drink alcohol, drink cold water from one of those expensive glasses from Tiffany. Exchange gifts, and flowers. Sometimes, talk about nothing—nowadays, problems of yesteryears or today or tomorrow seem to be the only subject of discussions, when folks talk to each other.

News flash ladies; if you don't want your partner to solve your problem, keep your fucking problem to yourself. "Women just want you to listen," is a bunch of bull in real life of today. If you continue to subscribe to the same mentality, your partner will begin to ignore you—that would be the beginning to the end of communication and connection. One more thing, men have emotions too. That doesn't make them mama's boy, most of the time; they are just human like the rest of y'all . . . Ok men, the same principles almost apply to you as well. Quid pro quo . . .

Forget the 50/50 in a relationship bull-shit. That was as old in a relationship theory as eight-track tape. Remember, everyone in a relationship has fundamental basic roles and functions to perform. Recognize your roles and follow them. Don't irrationally rationalize everything. Relationship is like the scale of justice, except it's not blind-folded. Open your eyes . . .

For goodness sake, erase the phrase "Love me for me," from your love dictionary. They don't mean shit if you want a lasting relationship. I stand corrected again, you will always find the "Rejects" to love you for you—pay his or her bills, buy his or her clothes, tell him or her how to breathe, especially him. I guarantee you; he or she will accommodate all the other shit you want. There is good news, if you can call it as such—your looser of a partner will support you, make you feel important, and let you be in control, until another moron, who is willing to outperform you comes around. Bank on it, there are many like you in the universe, ready to have any man or woman, at any price. I hope those over thirty something are reading this . . .

Remain young at heart. Remain young in age. Remain young in love making. Don't get old before your time. Use all legal means to enjoy sex to the maximum.

Remember, what goes on behind your closed door, within the four walls of your room, or anywhere you deem fit, is your damn business—not your mom's, not your father's, not your pastor's, not your friend's, not your teacher's, and surely not your damned nosy family members. Oh, forget about the nosy neighbors too, unless you would enjoy their presence, in any form.

Cherish everything that gives both of you pleasures. Do pleasurable acts as frequently as possible. Nurture

them. Add spices to your love and sex lives as often
as possible. Experiment with different love spices.
Remember, Americans do eat French fries, even
though; they were not created by Americans. Be
adventurous and be as nasty as you could. Caution:
always keep the good Book where you can easily
lay your hands on it, in case you have to pray for
forgiveness, after your nasty self. Trust me; He will
forgive you for whatever you did. He always does,
after all, He had seen it all.

Be a creative and progressive thinker in sex planning
and sex acts. There shouldn't be any shame in your
sex game. The only shame in your sex game is the sex
game you never played.

Do what it takes, by all means necessary, to make love
fun, romantic, exciting, and passionate. Don't dismiss
anything about sex until you tried it once and/or both
of you hated it.

Stop telling all your friends about your damn business
especially about your sex lives, unless they are your
family shrink. If you are having any sexual problems,
talk to your psychiatrists or watch Dr. Ruth's old
talk shows on YouTube. Even then, be careful. These
experts are limited by the extent of their knowledge
and experiences. They are not you. They will never be
you. At times, fuck their opinions about relationships.
For heaven's sake, wake up and know who you are
or who you ought to be. Discover who you are. Once
again, be real, for real.

Don't talk your partner to death all of the time. Take
cues from your partner before ranting. If you want
to talk about everything from the dead flies on the

windowsill to the kitchen sink, please, get a parrot, call your mother, call your pastor on the support prayer hotline, text your father, become a community volunteer, join the PTA, join any protest march, or call the psychic hotline. I wish you good luck on any of these; just don't talk him or her to death. Please, get a life . . . get a job . . . volunteer . . .

Don't expect your partner to fulfill everything you lack or want in your life. Learn to carry your own cross, some of the times . . . Jesus Christ did.

Remember that love and affection don't happen in a vacuum. Passion is the result of the underlying ingredient that germinated or created the love or sex you desire. After all, you can't enjoy a good meal if the ingredients are rotten. You can't enjoy a good relationship if the elements underlying your relationship are discouraging and depressing. Mutual understanding begets happiness. Happiness begets good relationship. Good relationship begets fantastic sex. Fantastic sex begets lasting relationship—that's the circle of love, my friends.

Never take love-making for granted. Love and passion must be cultivated, nurtured, evaluated, re-evaluated, fine-tuned, improved, and maintained. Relationship requires hard work—the reward is happiness, togetherness, and comfort.

Watch what you say to your partner verbally or otherwise. Love isn't an obligation—it's a mutual sharing of emotion, passion, companionship, and enjoyment. I have heard people tell their partners "Tell me what you don't like about me." This is a

rhetorical question because many folk don't want
to hear what you don't like about them. If they
reluctantly pretended they do, ninety nine percent
will do everything to defend their status quo. Instead,
observe your partner carefully and closely, to discover
their likes, dislikes, and consciously try to correct
the bad ones before your relationship takes the
wrong turn. Remember, nearly eighty five percent of
communications is non-verbal. Learn to pay attention
to each other's habits, needs, and priorities. For peace
sake, talk less and listen more.

I have three simple rules for you: control your temper
tantrums. Control your temper tantrums. Control your
temper tantrums.

Always remember this: nothing is new under the sun.
Sex is no exemption. If you can think it, someone
has done it. If you have done it, you're probably not
the first, and definitely, you'll not be the last to do the
same.

Go wild if you must. Scream if you should. Shout if
you have to. Remember to create memories for your
old age and during your old age. If you believe life is
too short, please, act like it.

Remember that all aspects of life's journey affect love,
sex, and love-making. Nothing in life in guaranteed,
therefore, make the best of it while it lasts. Death may
be certain in everyone's life but to a greater extent,
the timing of death or the type of death is left to the
individual's actions and reactions. Therefore, make
the best of your sex life, even if it won't last. Nurture
your love and make it better, one day at a time.

Draft your own marriage expectations in writing, apart from your marriage vows, with a two-year renewable option. Renewing such marriage agreement won't end your marriage, it may save it. Marriage for life is a myth in today's world. Go with the time. Long lasting or forever marriages are outliers. At the end of the two-year agreement, evaluate the problems and happiness, to-date. If the bad outweighed the good, dump your partner, especially if things are not working as specified in your marriage plans. You probably don't need the stress or anguish. If you don't end the unfulfilled union, the courts will do it for you sooner than later. Divorce lawyers will always be around to make loads of money defending both of you. By the way, the idea that married people live longer is all crap. After all, it was written, "What does it profit a man to gain the whole world and losses his soul?" Life is too short for that shit. Stop suffering in silence. Lest I forget, staying together to avoid alimony payments, division of property, and child support payments may not be worth the daily stress— one way or the other, you will pay. You are paying already by your unhappiness . . .

Don't behave like Angela Bassett in the movie "Waiting to exhale." In a scene, she burnt her husband's personal effects out of vengeance because her husband dumped her ass. If it happens to you, trust me, it may, sell such valuables at market value and use the proceeds to better your life: take a vacation, safe it for your children's education, go shopping on Rodeo Drive, or donate it to charity. Don't be stupid. Instead, be smart, and get even in a productive way on your way to the bank.

Anticipate and plan for separation or divorce in your efforts to find Mr. or Ms. Right. Even if you find the person you want or you think you want, the chances of separation or divorce are 60% in today's real world. Plan accordingly and reduce your stress when it happens. I guaranteed you, my friends, it will happen sooner than you think. Watch divorce courts on your TV or iPod for people like you . . .

Think sex, say it loud, do it good, and enjoy it to the maximum.

Remember, sex is never dirty.

Practice safe sex and good luck.

Her web site under construction is www.keep.sex.alive. forreal.com/am4u/2012

Ann Mary's children were fathered by former client or clients. She didn't ask for child support because she was loaded and wanted to accept full responsibilities for her actions. She was an independent woman by any definition. She actually became famous when one of her clients sued her for visitation rights because he believed one of her children belonged to him. His only defense was that the child's bow legs resembled his. A DNA test later proved otherwise. In fact, the child in question belongs to her only ex-husband, who was also a former satisfied client that left his wife the same evening their therapy session ended. She had seduced him during the so called intimate sexual therapy. He was fine and a Denzel Washington look-alike. He was in his late twenties and loaded with old money, Miami style of the seventies . . .

She had since vowed never to get married again. So far, she was enjoying the best of her world. Her sex-partners are now her office staff. She considered them her practice run.

One of her favorite office sex-partners was also a part-time punk rock musician with various artistic tattoos. Yes, she loved nasty boys, provided they could play any instruments, especially the talking drums and . . . She got that from her African roots.

CHAPTER 3

Sheila and Pat ate in silence for a few minutes until Sheila asked pat how the food tasted. "It's absolutely delicious, Sheila. The dish is my favorite," Pat answered.

"I'm pleased you love it dear. I made it especially for you. I picked up the ingredients this morning after our e-mails. There is more from me you must taste," she added.

"I'm flattered but you didn't have to do all that", Pat replied.

Pat was clueless about Sheila's intentions. She may be an educated lady; she was naïve at best when it came to seduction.

"Anything for you Pat," was Sheila's response. Sheila was playing everything slow and safe. So far, her plans were falling into place. To her, patience was the best strategy for success. She had waited five years for this moment, and God's willing, Pat was within her grasp.

Sheila stood and turned off the thermostat in the room. The temperature must have been 89 degrees even though the outside temperature was reading 65 degrees according to the latest weather channel on her IPhone.

After lunch or as Sheila called it, "Late brunch," each with chilled glass of white Riesling, the second bottle of the day, walked side by side, and occasionally stumbling into each other, as they took a tour of Sheila's pristine home. They both seemed a little tipsy and relaxed.

Later, they settled in Sheila's den and talked mostly about Pat's job.

"Pat, I never knew how you made it every day in that white men's club. I'm so proud of you. You're an inspiration to all women, especially to us sistas."

Sheila would've preferred to share her fantasies with Pat instead of talking about jobs or careers. For now, however, fulfilling her fantasies would have to wait. After all, everything was moving along as expected. So far, everything was working in her favor. What a smooth operator . . .

"Thanks Sheila. I probably couldn't do your job either. I wish my husband would bring our business and personal income tax returns to your firm. He had been loyal to the same tax accountant for the past twenty years. They were high school and army buddies."

Within a few minutes, Pat dozed off. She slept like a day old baby after sucking her mother's breasts. The wine might have also contributed to her status quo. The wine bottles they shared together were now empty. Sheila was sitting next to her and watching her like a hawk watching over her only offspring. She tenderly kissed Pat's forehead and gently placed her index finger on her lips and licked it. She then covered her with a soft-wool blanket as a loving mother would to her only daughter, born after six boys.

All that was going through Sheila's mind was how she wished she could spread Pat's sexy legs, gently massage her inner thighs, and slowly lick her labia, as she had done in her dreams many chilly nights.

"Sheila, be patient and control yourself. She will be my dessert and main course in due time," she told herself, one more time.

———————————•●•———————————

Unexpectedly, Sheila's husband opened the front door.

"Sheila, I'm hoooome," he announced, and walked towards the den.

Sheila scrambled, regained her consciousness from her day dreaming full of twisted fantasies and hope about Pat. She rushed to meet her husband by the door, almost crashing into him.

"You home earlier than promised, Ted."

"You're not happy to see me?" Ted replied.

She ignored Ted's question because happiness hadn't been in their marriage for a while and they both knew it. On his way home, Ted had stopped for the happy hour and his brain was already saturated with whisky on ice—175% proof. He had been abusing alcohol for sometimes due to the circumstances in his household . . .

"I was expecting you later and I'm about to start dinner," Sheila was speaking to him as if she was in the habit of cooking for her now impromptu beloved husband of the evening, even though she had not cooked for him in the last twelve weeks.

Sheila was just nervous. She recovered quickly, however, and said, "By the way, we have company."

"Who might that be?" Ted asked.

He walked to the den and saw Pat sleeping, under the cover, like an exhausted innocent child, after all-day backyard picnic activities, with friendly neighbor's children and playful pets.

As soon as he saw Pat, he immediately turned around, got his car key from the key rack, and faced Sheila:

"Sheila, you know how much I hate that bitch. I guess you didn't expect me home early as you said. You undermined my feelings, authority, and brought that evil thing into my home. Is anything going on between you two? Had anything been going on behind my back? Are you fucking her? How long have you been fucking the double-faced-lying-bitch? Is she your lover too? Did you fuck her today in my own house? Call me when she is out of my damn house."

Ted was too mad to wait for answers. He didn't want any. He wasn't expecting any, not from a traitor of a wife fraternizing with his enemy. He stumbled out of the house and closed the door behind him as hard as he could; he almost shattered the window glass panes.

"It's my house too," Sheila murmured.

The commotions woke up Pat. She immediately stood and was ready to get the hell out.

"Pat, I'm sorry you have to hear all that. Please, give me a moment to drop you off," Sheila said.

Sheila profusely apologized on their way back to Pat's car. When Pat got into her car, she said, "Sheila, I never blamed you, so let it rest. Thanks for the lunch anyhow. I enjoyed and loved it."

"This is for you, Pat. I hope you like it." It was a beautifully wrapped gift to her potential lover and friend. She was hoping there would be another day with her, very soon.

Pat immediately opened the gift. It was the same scented wool-silk blanket she had been covered with at Sheila's house. With a smile, Pat said, "Thanks Sheila, I love it, but I didn't get you anything."

"That's ok. Just promise me you will use it. I'm sure you will give me everything I need at the right time."

Sheila wanted to make sure Pat has a scent of her, every cold night. She later watched Pat drove away before heading home to face her husband's rancor.

Sheila knew it's going to be a hell night with her husband whenever he returned.

The evening might not be a waste, however. To her, the day was the beginning of many joyous moments she hoped, from her dream girl, Pat. She could feel it in her veins.

But first, in her soft and usual sexy voice, she called Pat to thank her for lunch and visit. She said seductively, "Pat, about your anniversary? I'll do it."

The day, time, and place were now set for the threesome wedding anniversary celebration. Awesome!

Pat immediately informed her husband, Paul T. Peterman of the good news with tempered emotion.

Pat told him with controlled smile, "Sheila will do it."

Paul just became the luckiest married man on the planet or among men who dreamt of such encounters as part of their sexual repertoire like Shakespeare's play, "As you like it."

CHAPTER 4

Sheila's husband returned home fifteen after one the next morning. He went straight to the liquor cabinet and poured himself another tall glass of his so-called suicide mix—three shots of dark Bacardi rum, two shots of virgin vodka, four teaspoons of orange juice, a dash of cranberry, tonic water, a teaspoon of freshly squeezed lime, and five teaspoons of pine apple juice, all poured over three crushed cubes of ice. He was a bartender in the marine. Unfortunately, no medals were awarded for such respectable services during his tour of duty . . .

Frankly, Theodore Samson was definitely ready for war with his wife. This time, however, he was about to fight a war with alcohol-socked brain. His self-ill-advised engagement is destined for a defeat.

Sheila was equally waiting to engage him for the final time. Unlike Ted, she was ready to confront the nightmare in her marriage with a clear mind. She was determined to win her war without a single bullet.

Her chat with him was a long, candid, and unfiltered monologue about their stale marriage, dysfunctional relationship, and unhappy co-habitation. Their marriage had been over for years. Sheila had had enough. Ted always refused to accept her resolve and his own reality.

In Sheila's mind, Ted's reaction for giving him a piece of her mind would be similar to throwing stone at a bird ready to fly. To her, she was ready to fly. She was ready to fly far away from a painful, unhappy, and stressful marriage. Had she not been schooled in the Queen's English, she wanted to say aloud," I don't give a shit no more."

She had refused to make love to him for sixteen weeks and counting. She remembered vividly the last time they had the stuff. It was on his last birthday, on a Tuesday evening, around nine o'clock, in her sewing room, when she involuntarily allowed him to "Do his thing." It was her last sexual gift obligation to him. She remembered the time because her children left with one of her so-called aunts to the movies at 8:50. The passion she has for him was gone. She had no regrets. Ted knew as much but didn't want to deal with the obvious. To him, divorce was out of the question. To her, divorce was the only answer.

—•—

Sheila was cool and calculated. Ted's judgment day had arrived, and boy, she let him have it:

> *Samson, you embarrassed me last evening. You insulted me with your typical jealous rage. You disrespected me by the way you spoke to me in the presence of my company, as if, I were your maid. Obviously, our conversations about respect for each other and our counseling on improving our communications in this marriage have not made any difference.*
>
> *You knew I was a lesbian when you met me. In fact, you lured me away from my roommate*

*and lover while I was in college. You told me
you would understand and support me, if
things didn't work out . . .*

*You wined and dined me. As a result, I had to
change schools to show my commitment to you.
I subsequently abandoned my lover to please
you.*

*You insisted, as you put it, "My pastor, the
good Lord, and my church will cure your
lesbian tendencies with the power of prayers
because you are too pretty to be gay."*

*I agreed after your insistence, which lasted
over one year, to love only you and bear you
the children you wanted so desperately . . . that
I believe I have fulfilled.*

*Even then, I never promised you that I would
never be with another woman.*

"But you wanted children, too, and . . ." Ted tried to interrupt.

"Excuse me, I'm speaking," Sheila fired back with a
controlled and calculated voice. There was no need for her to
act otherwise. She knew the end of their marriage is at hand.

*Unlike you, I was practically loyal to you
throughout our marriage. The little fun I had,
in your presence, was with your approval.*

*You've cheated on me multiple times which you
always considered forgivable and irrelevant
because you were away overseas during your
military service. You blamed your infidelities*

on loneliness, temptations, cheap happy-hour alcohol consumptions, served by tantalizing half naked slutty women, military service stress, and whatever reasons you could come up with anytime you were caught.

I deliberately and painfully ignored many of your affairs especially with my hairdresser-babysitter, Nykky, under my nose, in our bed, and twice in the closet of my daughter's room. My daughter told me about it when she saw the babysitter-whore fucking you doggy style. Your actions traumatized the poor child for years.

Till this day, you blamed it on everything, including unusual hot weather in Florida, your allergy to store brand laundry detergent, high gas prices, low gas prices, and President Obama's first debate with ex-governor Rodney. You were never short of excuses.

I knew about your one night stand with my secretary. You sure sabotaged and ended her marriage in earnest. Congratulations, lover boy!

I knew about your vacation in New Orleans with Caroline, our son's godmother. I was told you paid her to keep quiet. I also saw all her rent payment charges on our joint American Express credit card. I have copies of them here. You even maxed out the account in the process.

Ted, you couldn't hide your affairs as a smart player does. You are so weak to the extent that you can't even independently hunt for your own preys.

I have accepted your other son who is still with his mother in Chantan, South Korea, just as I had accepted your infidelity, mental abuse, and reckless sexual behavior.

And you wonder why your own children are not close to you? They never saw you as a father who cared or loved them . . . You embarrassed them with every move and turn you made.

Ted, when was the last time you touched me the way I wanted? When was the last time you ate my pussy like you used to before and after we first got married? When was the last time you gave me a bath as you did when you were courting and chasing me? When was the last time you let me reach orgasm? When was the last time you talked nasty to me during your so-called delicious fucking session, when I begged you to?

Ted, when was the last time you allowed me to ride your face when I told you it makes me reach orgasm faster? When was the last time you rubbed on me those fiery hot sex lotions I bought for me when you knew they made me feel sexy and romantic during sex? When was the last time you used my dildos on me when I begged you with tears? When was the last time you spanked me before asking? When was the last time we role playing, as we did, at the beginning of the fucking relationship? When was the last time you let me be me . . . ?

Ted, I'm not an idiot. I read your messages on your Facebook postings to and from Karlene who appears to be your daughter's age. I always thought you could do better. I now stand corrected. You and Woody Allen are probably cousins.

You stopped satisfying me a long time ago, Ted. I accepted your emotional abuse as my destiny and for the sake of our two lovely children I was happy to give birth to, but regretted being their mother.

I did my best to convince myself that I can be heterosexual with your prayers and all . . .

I know I'm by no means perfect in this marriage. However, I have sacrificed a lot for you and your career. I have moved so many times, to so many places, all over the world, I felt I was working for the Foreign Service. I practically lived in a suit case for you, while I put my own dreams and goals on ice.

I specifically remembered the time we visited Hedonism II in Jamaica on your birthday as you wanted, but you refused to allow anyone to touch me after I expressed my desires. You deprived me of anything I asked for. The least you could've done was to let me taste a little pussy. You never allowed me to enjoy a little freedom, and a little fantasy . . .

All you have done successfully was control me during this one-sided marriage. You've controlled me as much as you would a two-year old.

I've lived with you in fear and in bondage all these years. Sexual bondage, that is.

I've had enough, Ted. Today, I'm done. Today, I'm liberated. Today, I'm born again and alive according to my resolve . . .

For years, I coped with your arrogant cheap-beer-drinking ghetto-bitch forty-something-year-old sister, Maureen, and the rest of your dysfunctional family in the name of peace and family. I've had to pretend all was ok until I caught Maureen fucking your nineteen-year old nephew in our son's bed last summer during your family reunion. You then had the guts to scold her husband for sleeping with Maureen's first cousin. You knew both acts were sickening, yet, you only scolded your brother-in-law for his iniquities . . . y'all birds of the same feather . . . Hypocrite!

I hope you told your brother-in-law to get a DNA test to ascertain the father of Maureen first cousin's last son. Everyone is talking behind his back about the child's resemblance to him. No child should be raised without knowing his father's true identity.

You have made enough fool of me, Ted.

"But I did many things for you that no one could. I let you do what you like to do in my presence, and I . . . ," Sheila interrupted him and walked to the refrigerator for a bottle of cold water . . .

After a sip of water and a breather, she continued to speak over him:

> *No Ted, you listen. It's my turn to speak. I had listened to you over the years. It's my turn now to speak my mind, uninterrupted . . .*
>
> *I accommodated your so called buddies, especially your neurotic, overweight, ugly, stinking, beer-belly, and pot-smoking friend, Jacob, who had always wanted to jump my bones each time he came over here. He attacked me in our bed with his two inch, quick release dick program during one of your Sunday night football parties. He ejaculated before I could threaten to cut his weenie off with my sewing scissors. I can still smell his cheap cologne each time I think of his bad-breath-stinking ass.*
>
> *The only comment from you when I told you about the sad and disrespectful encounter was that he was drunk, and his actions were forgivable since he once saved your life in South Korea during a club fight with drunken locals. I bet it was over some whores y'all were passing around.*
>
> *Did he ever tell you, he gave me fifty four dollars and forty three cents on my birthday so that he could fuck my tits and lick my pussy? What a loser.*

By the way, he bought me that lingerie I wore for you on your last birthday. He told me it costs him two-week pay. Has his sorry ass caught up with his child support payments to his second wife yet?

Obviously, you don't know of an African proverb that says, "When your friend gives your wife an expensive present, it's time to get suspicious." You're so blind you can't even see an elephant in the room.

I had to stop attending your Pastor's prayer session because all he did was stared at my chest and constantly asked me to meet him for a drink at the church's dining room or at the altar saying, and I quote, "Work with me here, sista Sheila, before Elder Samson gets home." He once told me, and I quote him again, "If I fucked you and then prayed for your soul at the altar, you'll never think of another pussy again." When I told you about his harassments, all you said was, "You're hallucinating, Sheila. Pastor Covernor, III, was a man of God and a good family man." Good family man, my ass. I don't know about him being a man of God either. Ted, knowing all you know about him now, you seem to be the one hallucinating.

As of yesterday afternoon, I was free. I'm going to do me now. I'm going to make sure I get what I want.

But yesterday, you wanted to derail that prospect for me. Not anymore. Not ever, Mr. Theodore Samson.

Don't get me wrong, all was not bad between us, but so far, according to my record, my bad experiences in this marriage outweighed the good.

And finally, it's now clear to me today why you hated Pat so much. According to her, you guys dated in high school before you joined the air force.

You hid that fact from me, Ted. In a way, you and I will still be connected since the Pat you left behind will be mine alone soon. You miscalculated big time. I plan to possess who you used to have. For your information, she has now aged nicely like Californian 1971 vintage wine. Sweet indeed!

I'm going to have her if she would have me.

"My leftover and still a #@ii%," Ted interrupted.

Sheila cut him off once again and said, *but she is ripe, seasoned, and all grown up now.*

She took another drink of water and continued:

Ted, like I said, I'm done. We're done as a couple. Tomorrow, I'll discuss with my lawyer to go ahead and file the separation papers. Here is a draft for your record. I've asked for fifty percent equity in our residence and the same percentage for the other three investment properties. You can have the houses when all is done. I also asked for forty percent of your military retirement benefits, and $2,500 *monthly spousal support. The rest you can read for yourself.*

I need your cooperation in all of this because we are too intelligent to display our dirty laundry in public for everyone to see. Not that any of it matters to me anymore. But if that is how you want to play it, "Make my day." My lawyers will have a field day, I promise you that much. Ted, the choice is yours.

In case you care to know, my lawyers are the father-son law firm in Beach City. Your older sister once used them in her divorce against that African fellow you know so well. He paid handsomely. You too will suffer the same fate if you take that route, I guarantee you.

I'll speak with your daughter about all of this in due course and I'm sure she will understand. My son, or shall I say, your son will not be bothered until he gets back from school. He doesn't need the pressure right now.

I've no hatred for you anymore but contempt for your existence in my life. I just want a closure to my misery. You should too. Fair is fair . . . Everything was wrong from the beginning . . .

Before Ted could utter a word, Sheila stood, kissed him on his forehead and said; "Ted, I'm finally done with you in my life. Leave me the fuck alone."

With tears running down her beautiful face, she immediately went to the spare bedroom she had used for weeks. Never will she allow Ted to see her cry again. She had started the new beginning she wanted with Pat and nothing would tarnish that. Even if there wouldn't be a new beginning for her, she was finally determined to be free, like the birds of spring.

The slight thought of Pat had made her come alive. To her, Pat, was simply the best of them all. The thought of Pat had healed her wounds and soul. The possibility that she would be with Pat and make love to her was like manna from heaven. "Thank you Moses," she said aside.

She reluctantly sent Pat a good night e-mail message and asked her to give a shout out to her husband, Paul, and thereafter went to bed. She was pleased and fulfilled, the way she hadn't felt for a long time.

She opened her Bible and read some verses on peace, satisfaction, and happiness:

> *You make known to me the path of life; in your presence there is fullness of joy; at your right hand are pleasures forevermore. May the God of hope fill you with all joy and peace in believing, so that by the power of the Holy Spirit you may abound in hope.*

--------•●•--------

Still sitting in his den, Ted was speechless and defeated. The fact that his brain was partially soaked with alcohol didn't help either. He knew the end of his marriage was at hand. He wanted to accept the inevitable. He wanted to save his unhappy marriage. He thought about the holes in his life to-date, but refused to take responsibility for any of them. He recollected about his first love in high school but dismissed such love as a curse from above. It was the same love that ended his happiness at the tender age of eighteen until this day. It was a love too painful to remember. He fell asleep on the sofa and didn't wake up until one fourteen, in the afternoon. His son's phone call actually woke him up.

CHAPTER 5

Sheila didn't hear from Pat for nearly two weeks. She was frustrated, unhappy, disappointed, and wondered where she might have gone wrong to her dream girl. She had wanted to invite Pat for dinner again or spend a night out together as girls. She would have loved to possibly prepare breakfast for her one morning in bed. She was willing to take the relationship slow but anxious to get to her promised land in earnest. She really had no other choice, now that she had practically left her husband, her children, and her acquaintances, for good.

She was convinced; her husband might have intimidated Pat and scared her away. Maybe she should've met Pat at another place instead at her house until they got to know each other better. Or maybe, she shouldn't have allowed her to stay that long for lunch, including all that transpired, the first time around . . .

Every night before she drifted to sleep, she wondered why Pat had not called. She replayed many times in her mind the possibility that Pat was truly not into women as she had said.

However, Pat's previous invitation to be part of her husband's wedding anniversary gift to which she had already agreed, gave her a ray of hope. "Pat couldn't and shouldn't renege on that agreement howbeit verbal. There is still hope for me," she concluded.

Desperate, she called Pat over thirty times and could only leave messages on her voicemail until it couldn't accept any more messages. She became worried and helpless. She wanted to curse her husband again for contributing to her current debacle. She blamed herself for being impatience from get go.

One hot afternoon, she decided to find out why the hell her dream lover was missing for action. She wanted an answer for a dream that she so desperately wanted to come true . . .

Her office assignments were piling up and clients' appointments canceled. Her life was becoming meaningless—she had just separated from her husband and had put her faith in a one-sided love affair she thought was the real McCoy. She cursed her husband for possibly derailing her new found happiness. She blamed herself for ineffective and sloppy planning, the first time Pat came to her house, over and over again. Her plan A was definitely inadequate.

Everyone in her office was asking, "Sheila, are things ok?" Her own mother noticed something wasn't quite right with her every time they spoke on the phone.

"Baby girl, do you want to talk about it?" her mother asked her repeatedly.

"Just the stress of work mom," she constantly told her.

One Wednesday afternoon, Sheila told her secretary she would be taking the rest of the day and week off because she might be coming down with a cold or worse, the flu.

Upon leaving her office, she drove directly to Pat's office to ask her, face to face, why she was ignoring her and her calls. She was tired of guessing about Pat's state of mind. Then, she changed her mind and decided to just leave a note on her car. Alas, Pat's car was not at her usual parking spot. She denied she might be stalking her. After all, she had only driven by Pat's office thirteen times in six days. And on a couple of those times, she was pretending to avoid congestion on the Main Street, twenty eight miles away. That was her excuse and rationalization. What a liar.

"I'm not a stalker," she told herself aloud as if practicing her excuses, in case she might be charged with stalking or trespassing. Her love for Pat was playing games with her mind and soul . . .

She called Pat's cell phone one more time. Again, the call went directly to voice mail—it was still not accepting any messages.

Reluctantly she dialed Pat's office number only to be told that she was in an executive directors' meeting.

She felt even more betrayed, unwanted, used, unloved, disappointed, and lonely. She contemplated giving up and accepting her destiny but her infatuation with Pat within her bone marrow refused to let her give up. To any detached independent observer, she was possibly obsessed with Pat. The thought had crossed her mind; she just refused to face that reality, typical with many in her age group and circumstances.

As her last stand, she went into Pat's office and pretended to be her sister. She told the executive secretary, "I want to stop by and leave Ms. Peterman a message about our upcoming family events." Her note read: "This is your sis, please, call me. I'm worried sick. Your cousins missed you. Hope all is well." She made her note short and sweet, knowing full well the nosy, pretty boy secretary, might probably be wondering why he hadn't met his boss's beautiful sister before now.

The secretary was checking her out as she was writing the note to Pat. She knew he was looking at her cleavage. The poor twenty something office help might go blind the way he was concentrating on her chest. She always dressed to be noticed and desired. She actually dressed to kill that day, hoping Pat will see in real time, what she has been missing for weeks.

On her way home, her cell phone rang with unidentified number. She reluctantly answered, "Hello, who dis," with a voice as if she was coming from a divorce hearing where she had just lost custody of her beloved Poodle, Ruco, in a final divorce settlement.

It was Pat's voice on the other end. "Sheila, it's me, Pat. I hadn't been able to call. Accept my apology, please."

"I too have been calling, and couldn't leave any more messages. That was the reason I came to your office. I hope I had not overstepped my boundary," Sheila replied with a sign of relief.

"Shit, I almost ran through a red light."

"Are you alright Sheila? Pat asked.

"Yes babe. I'm fine. You are so sweet. I almost ran through the damn red light," she repeated once again. Sheila was almost crying. She knew Pat cared. She loved that about her.

"I'm glad you are ok. Sorry Sheila, I misplaced my handbag containing my personal cell and my laptop with your number. I had to suspend my cell phone services. At any rate, I just want to remind you that our fifteenth wedding anniversary is this coming Saturday, hope you're still game as discussed."

In reality, Pat was having cold feet. It took her almost two weeks to summon enough courage to go through with the plot she had organized and agreed to. She was nervous and at the same time looking forward to an event probably condemned by nearly all self-professed church going community of her faith or any faith on the planet.

Sheila smiled and said, "I'm ok with it Pat. Could we meet this evening at the café to go over the details?"

Sheila couldn't wait until Saturday to see Pat. It had been two weeks since she smelled her presence. She was resurrected, and once again happy like the first explorers who discovered oil along the coast of Louisiana.

"Why are you smiling, Sheila"?

"You really think so?" Sheila asked.

"Yes, I can tell you're, Sheila."

"Saturday is my birthday as well," Sheila said.

"Cool, it's going to be a big celebration all around. Let me run back to my meeting.

See you at the café."

Sheila was almost whole again and her plans to own and enjoy Pat, no matter how limited, were on schedule. She drove home like a maniac to get herself ready for her second date. She was keeping records. She knew the third date, coming soon, would be juicy and . . .

Sheila then reiterated a Nigerian proverb: Strategy is better than strength.

She had never doubted her resolve. She was just suffering from impatience and love of desire.

At this juncture, Sheila gave a sigh of relief and rejoiced in the Lord by recounting Isaiah 46:11:

> *From the east I summon a bird of prey; from a*
> *far-off land, a man to fulfill my purpose. What*
> *I have said, that I will bring about; what I have*
> *planned, that I will do.*

It was only Wednesday, and Saturday seemed a million years away. Sheila didn't sleep a wink on the eve of their third date. TGIF was all she said when Friday rolled along.

She went shopping. Victoria's Secret was her main destination. Nordstrom was another. She needed a few sets of stilettos, a few new bras, and a couple of new sex toys from the Eight Inch, Inc. She always traveled light. If her hopes and dreams had been marinated beforehand, she would have preferred to travel even lighter to see Pat.

Before entering the store, a middle aged, well groomed Caucasian gentleman followed her. She knew she was always a target of desire. Public admiration and attention had been part of her life since she could remember. She was cautious and pretended not to notice the stranger, as she walked into the store.

As she turned to her left to chat with the sales consultant, she ran face to face with the stranger. "Excuse me sir," she said sharply.

"I'm sorry Ms.?" he responded. He then went on to say, "I need your assistance, if you wouldn't mind, please."

"What might that be, sir?" she said.

The stranger couldn't believe how polite she was with her beauty. Admiring her beauty and manners, he said aside, "Maybe it was her southern upbringing . . ."

"Great. Today is my anniversary and I'm looking for something fantastic and sexy as a surprise gift for my wife."

"I don't think I can help you sir," she answered as she tried to walk away.

"Madam, I'm not a pervert. Here is my business card."

She took his card and perused it. On it, she read his name and his job title. The stranger was the chairman and CEO of an energy conglomerate Fortune 1,000 entity, headquartered in Energyville, Virginia. According to her quick analysis of him, he should probably be around 46 years old, highly educated from a properly managed public higher institution, happily married with six children: four boys and two girls, a Republican, and a player . . . or worse yet, he might be a gorgeous pervert with highly paid handlers that kept his dark side in the dark.

"Ok sir, I may be able to assist. What do you need?"

"Thanks. My wife is almost your size but not as gorgeous. Please select the most sexual and enticing pieces of items you would love to wear for yourself and your lucky man."

She smiled and almost flirting with him. She wanted to tell him, "Correction, pervert . . . I'm separated from my

children-daddy and madly in love with another woman . . .
I'm getting ready for a threesome in less than twenty-four
hours." But that would be too much information to a man
who was probably looking for a one night stand away from
his stuffy wife with vanilla sex life . . .

"Sir, how would you know they would fit her?" she said with
a smile.

"What's your name again, please?" the stranger asked.

"I'm Eboney," she responded. She just threw him a curve
ball. "All female black people are ebony—their symbol of
beauty," was the name the stranger thought he heard . . .

"Ok, Ms. Ebony, I know you have a good taste and you
wear everything well from all I have seen so far. I know you
pleased your man. I'll take a chance on your taste."

"Ok sir. Let me see what I can do," she told him as she went
shopping like an Ivy League graduate black professional
living in the suburbs of Washington DC, who had just been
invited by her friends to attend one of President Obama's first
inaugural balls.

Sheila took her time and selected the best in the store from
silk panties, silk tank tops, blue pajamas, white pajamas,
girdle belts; push up bras, chewable panties, collar belt, see-
through tank tops, accessible panties, demi-bra, five tongs,
split panties . . .

From the dressing room, she called the stranger, "I'm afraid
you can't see me in them but since you trust my judgment, I
think your wife would like what I've selected."

"Ebony, would you mind if the sales consultant takes a look at them and tells me her opinion?" he replied.

"Ok, let her come in, sir."

The sales person went in, looked Sheila all over, and reported back to the stranger as she was smiling like hyena, "Sir, everything looked gorgeous on her. I'm sure your wife will love them. Sir, I love them myself. Wish they were for me." For the first time in the life of the sales consultant, she wanted to be black for one day, just like Sheila, who had been created black, all her life, by the Almighty God.

The stranger smiled and asked the sales consultant the total cost of the items.

After punching some digits on her hand held calculator, she said, "Sir, are you sure you want all of them. They cost a lot." She took the total costs of the merchandise personal and excessive, as if she was the one shopping on her $8.15 hourly wage.

"Yes, I can afford them. How much?" the stranger said with a soft smile.

"Ok sir, I'm sorry. The total would be $5,967.96 after our 15 percent executive bulk-purchase discount for our valued clients."

The stranger paid for the items in cash and said, "They are for Ms. Ebony," and disappeared into the sprawling mall. "That lady was damned beautiful," he said to himself as he went to the pub, directly opposite the store, fifty feet away, for a stiff drink. He also wanted to have another glimpse of Sheila when she walked out of the store.

The stranger had watched Sheila, a.k.a, Eboney, as she entered the store. He loved the ways she walked with her tight butt. He loved her simplicity—clean and natural. Her makeup was light and stylish but sophisticated. Her nails were manicured without obnoxious colors or accessories. Her jewelries were simple and fitting; the color of her shoulder length hair was perfect and inviting. She was gorgeous, conservatively dressed, perfect body, perfectly shaped full black lips, and simply gorgeous.

In fact, Sheila would've been his dream girl any day if the time had been right. Too bad though, he was a corporate executive and married to a southern bell of a wife with new family money, from anything banking. Attempting to express or contemplate telling Ebony the reason he followed her into the store was out of the question. Deep down, he would've wanted to fly her, first class, to a weekend vacation at the Riviera, at any cost . . . He was so smitten by her beauty, he couldn't even ask for her phone number. If fate had been on his side, he would have loved to keep her as his mistress and trophy girl. But again, his female handlers (he calls them his public relations team) always made such social arrangements on his behalf. Unfortunately, they weren't around to do his dirty work on that day—his wife was in town, shopping away, spending her own money as if she owned the entire mall. She probably does.

When Sheila came out of the dressing room and wanted to pay for her own few selected items, she asked the sales person, "Where is that gentleman?"

"Mam, he is gone. These are the gifts he bought for you."

Sheila couldn't control her surprise. She had more gift boxes than those carried by Juliet Roberts in the movie, *Pretty*

Woman, on Rodale Drive. All she could say was, "Good Lord . . ."

On her way home, she was saying aloud, "I would've at least allowed him to see me in them . . . strange but a nice fellow." She hadn't been to church recently but she knew God was looking out for her, even at Victoria's secret, of all places.

CHAPTER 6

The day of Pat's celebration came. It was set for four o'clock that Saturday. The day started with a light rain but Sheila was ready to move by twelve after twelve. She packed neatly a few of her Victoria's secret Valentine collection for her dream lover, Pat. Nothing else was necessary. If there would be another encounter with Pat after the upcoming union for three, she would've preferred to wear only trench coat and stilettos.

She arrived one hour early. To her surprise, her hosts were ready and waiting. It seemed the sex party anxiety had attacked all concerned. Before she could knock at their door, the door's censor recognized her presence and was automatically ajar.

Paul Peterman, Pat's full-time husband until that moment, as history would later prove, welcomed Sheila by the door; gave her a bouquet of twenty-four long stemmed white roses, and a kiss on her right cheek.

With another kiss on her left cheek, he wished her a happy birthday, and said, "Welcome to our home."

Sheila followed him to the living room where Pat was sitting with her legs uncrossed and anxious to welcome her special guest. Pat was equally stunning like a new virgin, waiting to be united with her groom in a pre-arranged marriage.

Just looking at Pat, Sheila knew she was at the right place, at the right time, with the right members of the household.

She believed her dream had come alive. She was all smiles. She gave thanks for being born. For the first time in her life, she was proud to be born in America where freedom reigns.

Pat crossed her legs, then uncrossed them, and stood up to welcome her. Sheila could see Pat wasn't wearing any panties. Sharon Stone, eat your heart out. They hugged for almost two minutes and kissed briefly on the cheeks.

Sheila knew how to prep her preys. She touched Pat's smooth face and said, "Pat, you're a jewel and a beauty. Girl, you're stunning."

"Thanks. So are you," Pat replied with a smile from cheek to cheek. She was nervous but behaved like a pro. Silently, she started praying for her sins.

So far, all provocative actions were initiated by Sheila. She could be aggressive at the appropriate times, and on this occasion, on this union, on this rainy day, on this joint celebration, and on this joyful day for all, she would tread gently. She knew her fate and efforts had connected her to Pat and company. Destiny had brought new life, new hopes, and the happiness she always wanted. Pat has just become her manna from heaven . . .

At long last, Sheila concluded that her husband, Ted, was finally and emotionally history.

"May I take off your jacket, please," Pat asked.

"Sure babe. But you have to handle it as if you had just discovered your lost jewel," Sheila replied with a wink.

They both smiled, pretending to ignore the anticipated reasons they were all together for the evening.

Pat unbuttoned Sheila's jacket and was beautifully shocked and unexpectedly surprised to see that she wasn't wearing anything underneath her Italian custom-made grey wool coat. Sheila gently let her coat falls slowly to the floor. Sheila wanted to cut short the unnecessary pleasantries. Hell can wait. Shit, even if hell can't wait, she didn't give a damn.

In front of the wedding day anniversary couple was Sheila, standing in her birthday suit like a goddess with her 34DD: 30: 38 measurements.

For a few seconds, it seemed the electricity in the entire house short circuited. Paul swore he saw all lights blinked for a moment or two. Far from it, Paul's brain was just clouded after the combination of a few glasses of vintage wine and the divas standing in front of him.

Sheila's shoulder length hair was tastefully colored and perfect. Her lips were light chocolate, full, and succulent. Her 34DD breasts were light brown and firm like a soft papaya. Her nipples were pointed like baby cucumbers scientifically grown for a well-to-do vegetarian African foreign trained young Monarch. Maybe her hard nipples were as a result of the chilly evening breeze over a busty lady without an article of clothing underneath her coat, or it might be that her desires for the night were working overtime on her juicy juice mangos. Maybe her oxygenated red blood cells were rushing overdrive through the veins surrounding her nipples. Whatever the reason or reasons, Sheila wasn't expected to look that tasty and gorgeous after two young adult children. God's own creation was in full display. "Thank you Lord for your handy work," Pat said to herself.

As Pat bent down to pick up Sheila's coat, she saw at close range, how Sheila's pubic hair was well groomed. Her bulging pussy seemed ready for the occasion . . . Actually, every muscle in her body was ready to any naked eye without 20/20 vision.

Sheila gently lifted Pat up, hugged her, flesh to flesh, with deep and wet kisses. Her fresh soft body was pressed against Pat's shaking and weak legs. She knew Pat's body temperature had gone up at least 20 degrees. She could smell the aroma of Pat's moist labia and feel her clit throbbing. Pat was breathing heavily and out of character. Her palms were moist and shaking lightly. Pat closed her eyes as she enjoyed the moment, the environment, and their company for the first time.

------------•●•------------

The image of the third wheel in the room, Paul, was now clouded. The current scene was not intentionally part of Pat's plan. That was just how the game was playing out, so far.

Paul was speechless and hoping there won't be any uninvited guests tonight. "Whoever comes uninvited would be out of luck," he told himself. He walked to the window and saw that everywhere outside their home was quiet and almost dark. "Thank you Jesus," he said aside. Paul was actually nervous but thankful to his God for the opportunity to enjoy every man's dream. I stand corrected; he wanted to enjoy most men's dream.

Pat emptied her glass of wine and asked Paul for a refill. She needed the courage for the actions she had embarked upon. She was always a social drinker. This time, however, she was becoming a first time alcoholic with anything wine, made in the United States of America and south of France.

One aspect of the Peterman's family life would be anyone's envy. They did know how to enjoy life—they ate and drank only with china. Every meal was accompanied by a glass of good wine. They enjoyed caviar with imported biscuits from Europe. Paul wasn't crazy about the caviar. "I just wanted to eat the stuff because I could afford it," he would tell his friends. Once a month, they entertained their close friends in their Mansion with catered food and life jazz band. The sound of Coltrane or Miles Davis was their favorite.

On their annual one-month vacation, they had been known to travel outside the country: Jamaica, Costa Rica, St. Martin, Belize, Brazil, Mexico, Canada, to name just a few. Every other year, Europe was their favorite destination, including the Riviera. They had visited China, Taiwan, Egypt and her sister country to-date, Israel. Their most cherished place of all places where they had vacationed twice was the Vatican City. Yes, they saw Pope John Paul, IV, in one of their trips. Paul referred to His Holiness, as "My name sake in Christ." That was their only connection—thank you Lord.

Within the United States, they did most of their vacation driving their Cadillac Escalades to places like Niagara Falls, Martin Luther King's Memorial, national parks, Statute of liberty, and Hollywood. They had been to the taste of Chicago festival, Las Vegas, Disneyland, and the Lincoln Memorial.

As Sheila was erotically admiring Pat, Pat said aside, "I'm not like this nor should I feel this way."

"I'm all yours to have as you wish, babe" Sheila said in her usual sexy voice as if she was reading Pat's mind.

Sheila handed Paul her empty wine glass and said, "Paul, I need a refill, please."

Sheila bent down to pick up her own coat while consciously displaying her sultry 38 inch round butt.

Paul was now motionless at the door leading to the living room with a tray of ten full and chilled wine glasses for three: two for him, three for Pat, and five for Sheila. Paul didn't want to stop in the middle of any actions to pour or refill wine glasses. Every minute counts. What a genius. What a player. What a lucky soul.

Pat gestured to her husband, who was now standing frozen at the door, to close his mouth and breathe. Paul regained his consciousness, licked his lips, and forced himself to move forward. He offered his ladies the glasses of wine. Yes, he called his wife and their august guest, ladies now. At least, that was his illusion for the night. He had been blessed by two goddesses and he intended to enjoy them to the fullest, God willing.

Pat and Paul sat beside each other as Sheila sat across from them while Mile Davis' best played in the background.

———————————•●•———————————

Pat gave Sheila three white lilies, a card, and said, "Sheila, this is from me. Thanks for coming." That was their second gift of the evening to their special guest.

Shortly thereafter, they sang "Happy birthday" and Paul read verses from the card they bought for her. Sheila couldn't have asked for better hosts to celebrate her best birthday in years. To some extent, she felt safe and at home.

All of a sudden, Paul heard the front door unlocked. As he stood and rushed to the door, he said aloud "Sweet Jesus, who the hell is that?"

Thanks heaven, it was their housemaid sneaking out for the night.

The maid had miscalculated her exit timing for the evening before Sheila's arrival. However, she had her motive for the miscalculation. At the minimum, she wanted to see the special guest she had been preparing all the food and deserts all day.

To safe face and avoid any potential embarrassment, she retreated into the closet when Sheila arrived. She wanted to avoid being seen—she usually waited to give Paul a good night hug and a kiss before she went home each night. It was their secrets and, so far, they had gotten away with their puppy love affairs, if one could even call it that.

All the housemaid had been able to do since she locked herself in the closet was sent text massages to her cousin, who was expected to give her a ride home, telling her what might be taking place this night, at the Mansion of her employer . . .

"I'm sorry, Mr. Peterman, I was trying to avoid . . . ," she said nervously with some element of jealousy. She then added, "Do you want me to stay in case you want me to serve the food and deserts?"

"Don't worry about it, Angelika. Have a good weekend. See you on Monday (Monday emphasized)," he told her, as he locked the door and returned to his ladies.

"I thought Angie had gone home," he was saying to himself while rushing towards the den. He had forgotten the nightly puppy hug and kisses with Angie, who wanted to replace Pat, in Pauls' life. To-date, she would've had a better chance of winning the lottery with her delusion.

Paul announced to his two girls who are now entangled in the den, "It's only Angelika, Pat. We're good."

CHAPTER 7

The three that mattered, among the gangs of four, spoke at length about the current political environment especially the 2012 presidential election. Paul concluded that former governor Romney would definitely be the Republican nominee and would face President Obama for the 2012 presidential bout in November.

For the first time, Sheila interjected and said "Pat, what baffled me the most was the fact that President Obama never received any support from the Republicans, who for all practical purposes was their kind. The Republicans acted as if it didn't matter how their irrational and senseless opposition of him would affect the country or the economy, when in fact, Obama is actually one of their own."

"Why do you say that?" Paul asked, as if he had known Sheila for years.

"Well, Obama was raised by his white mother and her white parents all his life. From all indications, he has the same mind set and demeanor as the white folk. "No drama Obama" is an indication of his closeness to his true race—white. It's so ironic that Republicans give one of their own such hard times. Frankly to me, Obama is white by substance and African American by form. The Republicans are too naïve to see it. The Republicans probably knew the hidden truth, behind their closed door meeting, in room number 999, on C street, about affirming their uncompromising agenda because they are still sore about his victory in 2008 against their man, the great war hero . . . They still want the power and superiority they believed should belong to them exclusively, nothing more, nothing else."

Paul then asked Sheila, "Do you think President Obama will be re-elected?"

"Oh sweet Jesus, yes of course," Sheila replied.

Throughout the discussion, Pat said little. As a high ranking city official, she didn't want to be on record or misquoted. Already, she was nervous conducting a risky immoral get together as is. "What's going on in my house may be legal under privacy argument, but it's definitely immoral," she said to herself. She gazed at Paul and all of a sudden felt shy to face him. Paul smiled and urged them to drink up and quickly, in other to distort their state of mind. To him, patience was becoming a rare commodity. What a greedy man. But again, he was mortal.

Pat was now in direct conflict with her religious teaching as well. The spirit of her mother was probably cycling overhead, warning her against the devil among them. Nonetheless, she convinced herself that she was over eighteen, highly educated, married for fifteen years, and therefore concluded, she had the license to do whatever she so pleased.

Even though the 14.70% alcoholic content in her wine may be working overdrive, Sheila would have been her type if she were into women. She tried to rationalize the irrational. The irrational is winning . . .

One thing was clear; however, Pat couldn't believe how attractive Sheila is when she speaks. Sheila's lips curve with her words. Her knowledge and performances made her sexier. Turning her head with her flowing hair as she gestured even made her smoky, desirable, and wanting. People with brains always turned Pat on. Sheila would've been everything she wanted and much more, if she had chosen that lifestyle—she was sexy, intelligent, and physically fit.

If Pat hadn't known her husband for nearly fifteen years, she would've had reason or reasons to be jealous at the present time. Paul seemed more ecstatic, more alive, more connected to Sheila by the way he was looking into Sheila's eyes while his dick was growing by the minute as if trying to burst loose from his faded denim jeans. Paul made sure their guest and his semi-wife in-crime saw all of him . . .

Pat is having a second thought. Agreeing to let Sheila fuck her husband in her presence may not be such a good idea. At present, she had concluded all present may be going to hell anyhow. "I'll let her do me, at least," was all that was going through her mind. To her, the full figure of her husband's 7'.8" rod may be opaque but still visible at a distance. Maybe she was tipsy or hallucinating, she thought she saw her husband's dick in Sheila's hands or maybe in her mouth . . . "Whatever I saw didn't matter now," she said softly. She was already in the water and too late to be afraid of being cold . . .

"Lord, what am I doing?" was one more thought that came to her mind.

With refreshed glasses of wine on hand, they showed their gorgeous home, overlooking the Bay to Sheila. They showed her the renaissance chef-designed kitchen, their guests' rooms located at the far end of the house with the comment "We designed it that way for privacy." They also showed their sex playmate/guest for the evening, their bedroom, including a fire place next to an open bathroom made with Italian marble. They showed her the skylights over the Jacuzzi and all the surrounding tinted glass windows overlooking the Bay, where they can see out but no one can see in.

Sheila looked around and was pleased with her surroundings and commented, "Maybe I should just move in and enjoy the good life with y'all."

Paul's immediate unrehearsed response was, "We are ready any day and anytime you are ready."

"Sheila, Paul is joking," Pat said aloud while rolling her eyes at her husband.

Sheila smiled. She wasn't interested in cohabitating on a regular basis with them, not as a threesome anyway. She had been there and done that. Then, she thought to herself, "Maybe, it could be possible to move in if Paul moved out or if suddenly he was ran over by a bus."

Sheila sat on the edge of the Egyptian made bed, almost the size of a two king sized bed joined together. She was convinced without a doubt that she had arrived for the anticipated actions of the day. She wanted the occasion to begin in earnest. The clean, soft, and ten-pillow satin covered bed enticed her to want to fuck anyone right there and then: man or woman, Pat in particular.

Instead, Pat gently held her right hand and led her to their walk-in closet with special compact bed designed specifically for impromptu sex. "We built it when our cousins were young and living with us. We needed a hideout when we must have to have it. We never used it much," Paul commented. A hint to all present! The line he intended to use again at the right moment with Sheila.

On their way downstairs, Sheila was leaning on Pat for support or affection or the combination of both. At the middle of the spiral staircase, she turned and pinned Pat against the wall and kissed her with such passion that the wall seemed to move. Still holding Pat, she ripped off Pat's tank top, popped out her breasts and devoured her hard nipples like a calf thirsty for his mother's milk on a hot day. Within minutes, Pat's legs buckled and lost her balance. She was shivering and breathing as if recovering from a delayed orgasm . . .

Sheila looked directly into Paul and said, "Carry her and bring her to me in the den."

Sheila was now totally in control of her hosts. She was always a control freak. To those that knew her, her action shouldn't have been a surprise. She was the chair of the strategic control and logistics team of her firm. From all indications, she earned that title.

Around 6 o'clock, Pat announced that dinner should be ready in three minutes. Like an innocent virgin in the present of her fiancé, Sheila turned to Pat and asked if she could change into something more comfortable.

"I think I'm all wet under this coat," she was almost tempted to announce to her hosts. She also wanted to say aloud, but murmured, "Pat, wish you could lick me dry?"

Pat didn't hear a word of Sheila's side comments and instead said, "Please, go straight upstairs and you can use any of the rooms."

It had been twenty minutes and Sheila hadn't returned. By then, Paul was curious, impatient, and asked Pat, "What is she doing that took her so long?" "Patience, patience, Paul, she will be here before you know it," Pat insisted.

Paul turned to his wife and said "Babe, do you want us to go through with this? By the way, you look stunning tonight. To be frank, I'm nervous but I like her . . ." Before Paul could complete his sentence, Pat kissed him passionately; ripped off his shirt with such violence that Paul lost his balance and fell on the floor. Alcohol might be a catalyst to that imbalance. From there, Pat continued to kiss him, sucked his nipples, licked him all the way down to his belly button, and seized his hard cock that had stayed in full attention for the past one hour or so. Paul lifted and squeezed her butt with both hands and buried his tongue in her happy spot. He worked her pussy for nearly twelve minutes or less. In return, Pat pumped his rod with her right hand. With her sultry lips, she deep throated him like never before. To Paul, Pat seemed to be born again from within and alive. Miracle does happen . . .

The presence of Sheila in their house was already changing lives. Paul was like a Monarch from a small kingdom off the coast of Threesomedom, if there were such a place. In fact, there was such a place—their Mansion on the Bay, where the forsaken act is currently taking place.

Within minutes, they were lying side by side like two pythons during the mating season. They were moaning, as Paul was saying "Babe, don't stop. Never stop. Oh yes, I love that. Shit, I love it, don't stop. It has been so long."

With the corner of their eyes, they could see Sheila standing by the door and watching, but their hot and steaming sexual connection, and the fact that Paul was about to explode forced them to ignore Sheila's presence.

To Pat, things were getting better than planned. She was now relaxed and for the first time in over fifteen years, she enjoyed sex with her husband without an anxiety attack. For a second, she thought she should've agreed to do this sexual liberation of togetherness sooner. Of course, she was now under the influence of whatever she had been drinking. According to her record, she believed she consumed three glasses of wine, so far. Actually, she consumed seven glasses, counting the two forced on her by Sheila, by mouth to mouth transfusion, and the two glasses brought to her by rebranded husband, Paul . . .

From Paul's facial expressions, he must be thinking, "Pat honey, drink more, get loose, get nasty, and be free as a bird."

Paul couldn't lick Pat's pussy any longer because he was now moaning from Pat's full operations. He placed his dick tangentially outside Pat's pussy walls in order to prolong his orgasm, the second time.

Moments later, he entered her and exploded like a water pipe under enormous pressure. He was relieved. He was sexually satisfied. He was gracious. He was happy. "Thank you, Pat," he said. Paul's parents raised him well . . . he was always grateful after excellent services.

Without hesitation, Sheila took the baton from Paul, and joined the act. She knelt down in front of Pat, and devoured her pussy. She sucked it the right way. She licked it the perfect way. Thinking of Paul's performances, she said to herself, "This joker is an amateur. This pussy will always belong to me, anytime." Self-confidence was also one of her best attributes.

Pat moaned, pressed Sheila's head over her clit and rotated her tongue anti-clockwise and then, clockwise, with such intensity that Sheila could hardly breathe. Pat exploded. She didn't stop convulsing until all her jolly juicy flows stopped, courtesy of Sheila. "Waste not," was always Sheila's motto. Her mother taught her at the dinner table to always finish everything on her plate. This time, her plate was full of liquid aromatic juice and she deliciously finished its contents.

Sheila left Pat on the floor briefly and disappeared into the ladies' room. She later reappeared, refreshed like a model on the runway. Pat and Paul were pleasantly surprised and salivating over her new look, once again. She was wearing one of the items gifted to her by the strange gentleman she met at Victorian's Secret.

She walked in with her sexy six inch blue pumps with white lace panties, a red collar, and a skimpy bra unapologetically showing her full and bouncing cleavage. Red was her color, but she prefers white as a sign of purity. She also looks good in blue, green, purple, and black. Shit, she looks good in any color combination on the planet . . . She knew how to use and work her assets. For an accountant, she was one in a million among her peers. There was no specimen like her in her profession. In fact, few were made like her in any profession.

Sheila sat down between her hosts at the dining table, by design. They wanted all present to view the river from their $2,875,000 private driveway mansion, overlooking the Bay.

Pat turned to Paul, her current 50-50 husband of the evening festivity, "Honey, this is your anniversary present as promised."

Paul smiled and said, "Awesome, simply the best, and thanks horny. Sorry, I meant honey."

Paul stood and held out his right hand to Sheila. As she stood up facing him, he admired Sheila as if the black Mona Lisa had come alive. He led her to their bedroom upstairs. He wanted to lick Sheila's entire body like his favorite French vanilla ice cream on a sweet cone smothered with caramel on top.

The food downstairs was getting cold and wished the preparer/hosts and their special guest would take time to consume them. Sadly tonight, it would have to be eaten cold or probably not eaten at all. After all, none of the parties enjoying the anniversary day, could think of any solid food for the moment. They are already enjoying a bountiful harvest made of their body parts.

Uninvited, Pat followed them to the bedroom. Together, they slowly took off Sheila's skimpy outfit one piece at a time, as if archeologists were examining the remains of King Tut in his Tomb.

Paul wanted to palm Sheila's breasts but Sheila turned and faced Pat and said, "I need to freshen up." She wanted to extend Pat's anticipation. Shit, she was good. She was very good indeed.

"Right now and again, babe?" Pat almost said aloud.

Pat pressed a button on her iPhone and the shower turned on automatically. At the same time, the recessed lights preprogrammed to dim at dusk came on over the six-person green Jacuzzi, which was already bubbling with lavender, at room temperature. Angelika had set everything up as part of the preparation for the evening's special guest.

"Pat, give me a bath" Sheila said, as she was removing Pat's clothing.

The shower was ready. The steam circling the room was inviting. The organically formulated gel soap that would be used for this special union was ready. The scented minerals in the liquid soap besides the Jacuzzi exuded strawberry aroma as a result of the heat in the room.

Everything was waiting and ready to be used. Heavens, if only walls could talk. But the walls were screaming; the anniversary party of three just couldn't bother to listen . . .

The anniversary boy, Paul, joined then in the shower. He gently lathered up Sheila and assured that every contour of her body was delicately washed as if preparing it for future study by third year medical students. Sheila turned to Pat and started to palm her breasts while licking her razor sharp nipples.

Not to be out done, Paul knelt between the two hot divas and made all efforts to suck Shelia's nipples. He had no luck. The available space between his girls was too tight. The participants were too clinched together as the music of Teddy Pendergrass, *Turn off the lights* was playing softly at a distance in the living room downstairs.

If this togetherness had been planned for three, only two had become relevant. The only two people in the ring for the friendly match were now Sheila and Pat.

Paul had become the third wheel by default. That wasn't in the original plan. And again, plans do change as circumstances change . . . Paul ought to know better, he was in the construction business . . .

Sheila was enjoying what she had hoped for with Pat. Pat had momentarily forgotten her official sexual orientation. She wasn't really confused of her identity; she was just ignoring her reality for the moment. "If I would be going to hell, I better start in earnest," she convinced herself. She had concluded, she would receive the same judgment and punishment regardless of the length of time she had sinned.

It seemed the adage, "Don't knock it before you try it," was now applicable to Pat.

When the story about the affairs of this day is written, the title would definitely be "The taming of the doubtful."

The only benefit Paul received so far with act two, scene one, was observing the mixture of Sheila's juices oozing from its source and down her thighs.

Paul was now "The watcher." He almost said to Pat, "Shit, it wasn't supposed to be this way." And again, beggars have no choice. He wanted a bite of Sheila, as such, he must be patient. After all, good things come to those that wait. "The night was still young," was all that was running through his head . . .

Then he recollected 1 Thessalonians 5:2: "For, you know very well that the day of the Lord will come like a thief in the night." That night was February 5. Sheila was the thief of the night, coming for Pat. The house invaded would be their Mansion on the Bay.

The two ladies finally rinsed and Paul dried them up one at a time. As Pat walked over to the Jacuzzi, Sheila turned to Paul and lifted one of her legs over the Jacuzzi base and said, "You can lick my pussy now." Paul obeyed. He told himself over and over again, "Yes, she must be obeyed."

After Paul thought he had fully licked her pussy to her satisfaction or maybe Sheila closed her legs to signal that she

had had enough from the anniversary boy, he led her gently
into the Jacuzzi that was already bubbling in fragrances.
The water temperature was at the right degree: 66.89. It had
been preset accordingly. "Money talks, some of the time. It's
always sweet to have it, unlike the 47 percent of the country,"
Paul said to himself.

He carefully studied and admired Sheila's entire contour
like a devoted mother admiring her only daughter on stage
performing Shakespeare's play "The Taming of the Shrew".
He rubbed Shelia down with lavender from the orient, as he
watched her facial expressions to ascertain that he was doing
everything right. He was able to do to Sheila all that Pat
refused to appreciate from him . . .

Paul had one great attributes—he loved to please his women.
I beg your pardon; he wanted to please his invited guest of
the evening, Sheila. Pat just never warmed up to his crafts
until this special day. Maybe competition begets jealousy and
jealousy begets openness. Openness definitely begets nasty
sex this night, on this day of our Lord, February 5. Cool . . .

Sheila made it worthwhile for him too. She licked her lips and
slowly spoke into Paul's right ear, as she bit it softly, "Are you
enjoying yourself, anniversary boy?"

Paul lifted up Sheila and directed her to sit on his face so that
he could be in a better position to lick her clit like the pro he
wanted to be, and anxiously wanted to prove.

He was in a hurry. He wanted to be in a hurry, since he knew
there may not be another chance or another day, with the best
lady he ever had. He wanted to try many fantasies he could
not discuss or share with his own wife. He had wanted Pat to
grind her wet pussy over his dick, slid it over his belly, and

then rested it over his face in a see-saw movement. Pat had never wanted any part of it.

Maybe Pat was a victim of her religious upbringing—she belonged to the other religion. Definitely, she wasn't a Protestant. He would like her to reevaluate her faith after the ceremony of the evening.

Pat was getting jealous of the attention Sheila was giving to Paul. She was jealous graciously as she watched their consented adultery taking place in front of her and their maker, Lord Jesus Christ. She had finally accepted as her fate, that she would be going to hell sooner than she thought, because in the presence of her Lord, she knew she had sinned. Her only consolation was her recollection of one loophole: Jesus Christ died on the cross for her sins. "Thank you Lord," she said with a sign of relief. Deep down, however, she also knew she might not qualify for the broad God's forgiveness of her sins this chilly evening because her sin wasn't one of the assumed forgiven sins on the cross.

In the eyes of any decent humans of her generation, she was guilty. In her soul, however, it was the best of time. She was in little heaven at the moment. Again, hell can wait, since heaven must wait for the faithful.

Paul, on the other hand, didn't give a damn either way. To him, he was equally in heaven on earth. He would deal with his hell later. He immediately rationalized his action and convinced himself by saying silently, "When I'm in hell, no one I know will be there to witness it anyway." He forgot God's omnipresence. Yes, he read the Bible; he wasn't just convinced about God is everywhere part, not this evening of his full erection, ready to damage anyone that comes to pass. I beg your pardon, not this evening of their celebration . . .

Sheila noticed Pat's dilemma and gently said, "Pat, I thought you only wanted to watch? I'm doing what you wanted. Honey, don't be mad."

Pat had no defense. She turned and pretended to be powdering her nose and adjusting her bra in front of the wall-to-wall mirrors in the bathroom.

Paul then asked Sheila, "Could I lick you all over for a spell, please?"

"Shit, this man loves to lick," Sheila said, as she turned him down again. She then said, "Don't be in a hurry, we have all night. I've plenty of me that must be pleased by y'all."

CHAPTER 8

Barely clothed, Pat went downstairs to get the following ingredients: caramel syrup, French vanilla ice cream, a stick of refrigerated lollipop, a shot of whisky, a can of whip cream, a spoon, a bow full of ice cubes, and a small bow of olive oil, at the request of Shelia, blessed by Paul.

The time was now around eight o'clock. "Damn, the time is going fast," Pat said aloud.

On instinct, on her way back upstairs, she turned towards her front windows. To her surprise, she observed unidentified car parked besides Sheila's, on their driveway, with only its parking lights on. She knew it didn't belong to Angie, the housemaid, who temporarily interrupted their gathering early in the evening.

She immediately rushed to the bathroom upstairs where the pre-arranged God-forsaking sex marathon was taking place between Paul and Sheila, and announced that a strange car was parked outside their home with the parking lights on. "I don't know who the hell it belongs to," she nervously said.

Seeing how Paul and Sheila were getting it on, in her absence, she became slightly jealous. Running through Pat's mind was, "I thought Sheila preferred women."

Pat had refused security for the weekend. She wanted to be alone considering the evening's arrangements and agenda.

Paul reluctantly disengaged from Sheila. While walking towards the upstairs' window, he was cursing the uninvited son-of-bitch who might be trying to obstruct their evening's merriments. He thought it might be the housemaid's car still waiting outside to be nosy. It wasn't the maid's. He couldn't identify the car either.

It was Sheila's turn to ascertain the car's identity. Sheila ordered all lights dimmed because she was naked and unfamiliar with the neighborhood, even when the next door neighbor was one block away.

"Shit, its Ted's car." Sheila announced. "You husband?" Paul reiterated.

Within minutes, her husband, Ted Samson, shouting on top of his lungs, was knocking at their door. All the three parties upstairs froze and speculated how to handle the situation. The presumed man of the house, Paul, directing everyone not to answer the door said, "The idiot would leave if no one answered him." He didn't even know Ted that well to be calling him names. Well, that's how things usually turn out under these circumstances—the innocent gets blamed for the crimes committed by the guilty.

Sheila then sat on Paul hard dick without penetration, and started to palm and suck Pat's robust brown breasts.

"Pat, I never told you this, I've admired your boobs for a long time so much so that they keep me up many nights. I love the way they bounced gracefully. Your walk makes my pussy wet every time I think of it. I would love to ask you for a picture of those melons for my screen saver. They are simply gorgeous. They are simply the best. I hope you will give me the opportunity to worship them more frequently from now on," Sheila told her.

Sheila's analysis of Pat's breasts was on target. They had been the object of discussion in many circles. Friends and foes alike assumed Pat had had breast argumentation for her breasts to look so perky, full, proportional, and delicious to any sight. She had told every admirer the truth that they were real and blessings from God, each time she was asked to refer them to her plastic surgeon. To-date, no one believed her. Everyone with twisted fantasy will never believe her. She wasn't even from the great state of California for anyone to think of her like that. What's more, those with normal fantasies would probably give up their citizenship to have a piece of her bonbon.

Her husband also had a share of his own explanations to his friends about his wife's perfect breasts and round butt. His drinking army and/or college buddies talked about her beauty to his face, how he has been able to handle his wife's double blessings he took for granted. Although, he found the comments offensive, he couldn't do anything about it. As he sees it, they were haters, he tried to convince himself. In reality, they were not haters; they just admired beauty when they saw one. They wished such beauty belonged to each of them exclusively. They will trade their wives for Pat any day. They were all sad souls . . . greedy souls . . . twisted minds . . . perverted souls . . . but all God's children and humans, nonetheless.

Before Paul and Pat moved to their current private driveway mansion, many admirers drove by their house just to have a glance at Pat's chest while working in her flower and vegetable garden. Many took a stroll around her house pretending to be good neighbors merely to have a glimpse at her perfect body.

In their current Mansion, many just drove by, at a distance, just to know their dream and beauty was residing inside the Mansion. The thoughts of her residing in the abode were soothing to their lonely and wanting souls.

In a way, her gym membership had paid off too. She had maintained the same physique for the past ten years. Her personal trainer, Dana, would have performed his services free of charge any day and anytime to be closer to her more times than necessary. Sadly thought, he wasn't her type—he was dark-skin, bald-headed, big flat nose, average height, talks too much, college dropout, and used too much cologne.

Two years ago, a local talent agent had approached her for collection of her photos. He told her that he could pitch her portfolios to magazines and model search agencies across the country. "Who knows, Playboy might come calling. There is none of your kind since the days of Vanessa Williams," he told her.

She never wanted any part of it. "I'm not interested, Hugh Hefner Empire would just have to wait," she gracefully declined. Pat had more traditional and political career agenda in mind.

Ted continued to pound at their door, saying "Sheila, I know you're in there, open the damn door right now. I'm not leaving until I speak to my wife. I know what is going on there. All of y'all should be ashamed of yourselves. I saw the light dimmed as I was about to knock on the door. I know y'all doing something nasty and ungodly in there. Open the damn door, Sheila."

The banging on the door was becoming louder to the extent that the next door neighbor, a block away, could hear the echoes of his ranting and knocking.

Paul didn't factor in the interruption in their celebration plans that night. "Ted of all people," Pat reiterated, with a smile.

After disturbing the peace and interrupting their plans of the evening for over fifteen minutes or so, Pat had had enough. "I had enough of this shit," she said aloud. She got up and said, "I got this," and walked directly to the front door with only a thong and a red velvet bra made from an imported French cut, barely covering her succulent breasts. She was prepared for the unyielding individual she had prayed to forget for most of her life.

She gently opened the door and said to Ted, "Mr. D.R (Date Rapist), have you forgotten that? You're trespassing on a private property. Sheila is our guest and she doesn't want to see you. Please, leave immediately."

"Boobsy, I've no business or problem with you. I just want to talk to my wife. Sheila is still my wife, for your information," Ted replied, ignoring the nick name, D.R, Pat had just called him.

"Like I said, you must leave immediately," Pat replied emphatically.

It was now getting clearer why Pat agreed to invite Sheila as well. Revenge, was the greater part of it. However, she might have forgotten the Chinese proverb that says, "Those who want revenge must dig two graves."

Pat closed the door in Ted's face, punched some digits into
her official cell phone and within minutes, five police officers
(three men and two women) were breathing down on Ted's
neck with their guns drawn before he could say, Bagdad and
the name of the 43rd President of the United States of America.

A 299 pounds, salt and pepper-hair police inspector in-
charge of the response team, hardly finished reading Ted his
Miranda rights, before two other male heavy-set officers,
who could each bench pressed 580 pounds easily, forced him
to the ground. He was handcuffed, placed under arrest, and
charged with countless offenses under the sun, including—
terrorism, trespassing, invasion of privacy, disturbing
the peace, aggravation, theft, defacing private property,
resisting arrest, insulting the officers of the law, mayhem
of police officers, intoxication in public, public nuisance,
operating a motor vehicle without a valid driving license,
driving a vehicle with expired inspection sticker, expired
tag, and cracked windshield. In addition, he was charged
with possession of narcotics (he threw out a bag presumed
to contain illegal substance when he saw the police), rape,
possession of a deadly weapon, (evidenced by the jagged edge
found at the glove compartment of his car), driving with half-
empty whisky bottle, driving with empty cans of beer, and
illegal parking on private property.

Many more charges might be added later, he was advised.

Pat was the city's acting chief of police. Obviously, Ted had
messed with the wrong woman. He had come to the wrong
house and crashed a private party without formal invitation.

Ted had finally come face to face with his past, one more
time. As he was hauled to jail, his 2011 SUV BMW was
impounded, on the directive of Pat, and towed to the police

crime facility to search for further evidence. Pat didn't want to see his car on her property.

"Ok guys, we are at peace now" Pat announced to Sheila and her part time husband of the evening. By then, their sexual urge had cooled down a little and everyone's temperature was back to near normal. Nonetheless, their entire house was full of pussy juice aroma.

"Maybe, this was just the break we needed to finish our dinner," Pat said.

Sheila volunteered to finish serving dinner to the wedding day anniversary hosts in her skimpy attire with her green stilettos. So far, she had changed her clothing five times during the evening. She sure knows how to turn on the heat. She made sure Pat wasn't neglected and uncomfortable. To this end, she pretended to be ignoring Paul and kissed Pat on her forehead and said "Pat, let me serve you too, after all, you're the better half of the fifteenth wedding anniversary."

Sheila picked up a well marinated boneless chicken nugget with two fingers and fed Pat. She made sure Pat licked sultrily her fingers with the horny baked nuggets.

Sheila then brought out two wraps of cannabis, lit one and said, "See what Paul found outside the front door. Ted might have thrown them out before the 'Popo' arrived."

She shared a couple of joints with Paul alone.

Pat never touched that stuff but had become a second hand-smoker by her husband and company. Within minutes, she was flying high after inhaling the cloud of the cannabis. The three celebrants were pleasantly joyous. It's worth repeating, they were fucked nicely . . .

The wine was flowing, the music was playing, and the atmosphere was becoming cozy, alluring, and fantastic. Out of nowhere, Pat asked Sheila for a dance. They danced close, cheek to cheek, as Sheila skillfully kissed her on her lips.

Then, Pat with a weak and hardly audible voice looked directly at Sheila and said, "Sheila, you know I'm not into ladies and . . ."

"I'm not ladies, I'm your one and only lady, Pat," Sheila replied.

They kissed like there was no tomorrow. Sheila skillfully caressed her soft and silky skin, bit her ears lobes lovingly, and rested her tongue on her hard nipples. She sucked each breast interchangeably like a thirsty and hungry six-month old male child sucking his mother's bosom.

To ante her performances and to be the best she wanted to be to Pat, she evoked her uncle's words, "Life is hard, these are tough tits, but somebody got to suck them all night and sometimes half of the day." Sucking Pat's breasts, she did. Palming her breasts, she did, like a breast examiner at a medical free clinic.

Paul enjoyed the scene playing out right in front of him for a brief moment. He joined the couple on the dance floor. He got behind his wife with impromptu massages and knelt down to kiss her belly button.

Being the pro she is, Sheila calculated Paul's next move or what his next move should be. She started to finger Pat's vagina to get it moist, hot, juicy, wanting, and ready for the pleasure of the two beneficiaries present.

When Sheila knew the time was right and Pat's body was ready again, she did one of the Hollywood music super stars' act and lifted one of Pat's legs over an overturned chair and commanded Paul, "Get on your knees and lick her now." Paul obeyed. Pat was moaning loudly as she unbuttoned Sheila's bra with the energy left in her. She started to palm Sheila's breasts and sucks her nipples like a thirsty teenager would for the first time. Pat reached orgasm as she held Sheila close, tight, she almost broke her ribs.

She left an indelible mark on the back of Sheila with her manicured finger nails. Shit, Sheila wanted more . . . She always enjoyed a soft S and M.

For the first time in twenty years after her rape, Pat was having sex as it was meant to be. Like a virgin, she wanted it. Like an innocent nineteen-year old, she enjoyed it. Tears were running down her cheeks, as she turned to her husband and said, "Paul, make love to me for the first time."

He did, even though he never understood why on earth she would say, "Make love to me for the first time." The new discovery about his wife will be resolved in due time, and not on this joyful night.

Pat held Sheila's hand, winked at her husband, and led both of them to the bedroom where they resumed their sex escapade. This time though, Paul took charge. He put on his condom, turned Sheila around, and penetrated his entire 7'.8" rod inside her asshole. It was a perfect fit. Paul's penetration was a little painful, but very much desired by her. It has been a while since she had the full effect of a good dick. Dildo wasn't a substitute by any means.

Pat was now watching as she wanted or as she originally planned.

As Paul was riding and pumping Sheila doggy-style like a wild dog, Sheila beckoned to Pat to lie on her back. She then pulled Pat's hips to the edge of the bed for a better view of her pussy. "Open wide, and let me pleasure you as you deserve." She joyfully began to prepare Pat for the best feat she would ever experience.

All of a sudden, Sheila's cell phone rang with a familiar ring tone. It was her daughter. "Hi mom, what happened? Dad just called me collect that he was locked up and said you and some lady did it. I'll be home in a couple of hours, mother."

"Guys, I have to go. I would've loved to spend the night and make breakfast for us. Pat, keep that pussy warm and I'll take care of it at the right time," as she was gathering her belongings. In a way, she didn't want to lay all her cards on the table for Pat in one night anyway, even if she hadn't received the phone call.

Pat was still laying on her back, shaking from orgasm, excitement, and wondering if "I'll take care of it at the right time" would be sweeter than what had just happened to her.

Paul walked Sheila to the door, kissed her forehead, gave her his business card containing his cell number, and said, "Sheila, thank you for coming, drive safely, and hope we can do this very soon."

Sheila drove home with the thoughts of two worlds. One world was full of fantasies, desires, and hope. The other world was about her family she wanted to leave behind. Both worlds were about to collide.

Sheila welcomed home her daughter. They spoke until dawn as she explained the events of the evening, except the threesome that had just ended forty-five minutes ago.

For the first time, she told her daughter of her sexual orientation and the sacrifices she had made in the marriage for the sake of her family. She told her how she had sacrificed her happiness and gave up many things her heart desired because of her and her brother. She spoke with tears about the pains she had endured. Not from physical abuse but from mental abuse, emotional abuse, unfilled sexual freedom, and the consequences of her lifestyle . . .

Even though her husband had been a model husband in public, she had been deprived the peace of mind she deserved, the true love she was endowed, and the lifestyle she wanted.

Mother and daughter hugged, cried, and promised to love and support each other.

"Mother, this will not be easy for all of us, but I'll support you in whatever decision you make," her daughter told her. Like her mother, she was in pain, to say the least.

Sheila called Pat before taking the early morning nap. She was exhausted and needed to hear Pat's soothing voice. Paul answered his wife's phone and told her that Pat was already asleep and delightfully exhausted. "Thanks for everything and hope you enjoyed yourself today. I really hope we do it all over again soon," Paul said.

"Great. I hope you enjoyed yourself as well, Puky." she answered.

Paul now has a nickname: Puky.

Yes, Sheila already knew there will definitely be a next time, not with Paul as cohorts. She knew without a doubt that Pat would be the exclusive recipient of her love and nasty-self, if there is another opportunity to be with her.

"You had your only taste of heaven buster," she said to herself about Paul as she hung up the phone.

CHAPTER 9

The next morning, the District Attorney for the city of OldPort concurred with all the charges levied against Mr. Theodore Samson and agreed to prosecute him to the full extent of the law.

After ten days in jail, Ted was out on bail. He realized after meeting with his lawyers that it would be a hot winter for all concerned. He had finally jumped over the cliff; he just wasn't sure what his physical and emotional condition would be even if he survived the impact.

For his bail, he signed the following agreements with Sheila and Pat respectively:

To Sheila:

First: He would move out of their home immediately and live in one of their vacant rented investment properties and assume its mortgage and maintenance expenses.

Second: His bail money would be subtracted from the equity distribution of their real estate holdings from the final divorce settlement—he must pay for his crime out of his own share of equity distribution.

Third: He must not come within one mile radius of Sheila at all times. If they met by coincidence, he must change course immediately.

Fourth: In "He must be" family gatherings, such as graduation, weddings, a death in the family, he must obtain permission from Sheila and his social worker ten days before such event(s) for a planned supervised visit.

Fifth: He must sign the separation papers he had refused to sign to-date.

Sixth: He must obey the gag order and not speak to anyone about the arrest or the events that caused it.

Seventh: He must attend 40 hours of anger management, 150 hours of community service, and 40 hours of AA meetings.

Sheila got all her demands and more. Mr. Theodore Samson's bail was set at $250,000.

His lawyers protested against the agreement as unfair and prejudicial. They also failed to convince the presiding judge who reminded Ted in no uncertain terms, never to mess with high-value government official, next time around.

Pat on the other hand, would agree to drop the charges of rape, theft, and mayhem of police officers, if Ted agreed to the following:

To Pat:

First: He must stay 350 yards away from her house at all times.

Second: He must stay 1,000 yards away from her office anytime of the day.

Third: He must stay 150 yards away from her anywhere else she might be performing official functions. If by any chance, they crossed path, he must change direction immediately.

Fourth: He must obey the judge's gag order and not discuss the arrest with anyone.

Fifth: He must write an apology letter to Pat for the date-rape while they were high school sweethearts and pay up to $11,600 of her therapy costs.

Sixth: He must pay for the damages to Pat's car on the night of his arrest.

In addition, Pat, with the recommendation of the district attorney, refused to drop the narcotic charges.

After three days of back and forth negotiations between the lawyers, Ted signed the "Get out of jail" agreement with Pat.

He had pissed off the wrong woman, and maybe, Pat had finally awakened the sleeping dog.

When all is said and done, all parties had hoped none of that day's events had happened. Their lives would never be the same. What a pity.

Ted's date rape charge deposition was disclosed in details (the transcripts were about 588 pages long). Contained in the deposition was the fact that Patricia Morgan Suckleford (Pat) and Theodore Samson were hot items in Victory High School. It was nearly 20 years ago when their affair began.

Pat and Ted started dating when they were fourteen. They bonded the first day they met. Pat had the love of art, physics, and was the captain of the cheerleaders of her high school's Sugarcaine football team.

On the other hand, Ted was an aspiring baseball player with a passion for math, biology, and girls. He was very popular with the girls at Victory High. Pat overlooked his collection of girls because of the way he first approached her.

He had come to her in the school cafeteria and simply said "I want to be yours if you would consider having me." He gave her his little black book and said, "It doesn't matter what you do with it but I've reached the end of my search now that I met you. I'm in love with you, Ms. Suckleford."

Pat never wanted to date a jock. She was fascinated with geeks and anyone with science enthusiasm. Most importantly, she fell for Ted because they were born on the same day.

"That was profound for a 14-year old," she told herself. The fact that he knew her last name after she had thought for months, even with her beauty, she wasn't in his league, made her fall in love even more.

They dated on again and off again after that. They were on, most of the time. The only problem was that Pat refused to have sex with him. Heaven knew, they did plenty of kissing, and fondling numerous times, he had wanted to have sex with her. During foreplays, he ejaculated so fast before she could suck his nipples for two minutes while stroking his cock.

She didn't want any sexual penetrations, period.

According to her, she wanted to keep her virginity until marriage. She wanted to go places and no man or sexual pleasure would stop or impede her dreams. What's more, she came from respected parents with religious devotion, faith, and commitment. She wouldn't do anything to disappoint them.

Pat's father was a man of few words, but effective. All the birds and the bees' father-daughter moment he ever told her was, "Pat, you know I love you and you also know I'll do everything in my power to support you, but once you decide to be with a man and get pregnant, then, you have told me plain and simple that you don't need me anymore."

The talk worked until Ted violated her. All Ted wanted all along was to taste her juicy juice, violated her virginity, and win a trophy to show his friends of his conquest with the most beautiful girl at Victory High.

During their many separations, Ted had had sex with one of Pat's first cousins. She was a 20-year old student, majoring in "TV reality show management," at a community college three miles from his high school. Ted confessed his version of the affair to Pat in a letter the day after. That was his story.

They were both in love. He promised never to do it again. She forgave him but probably never forget. Unfortunately, he was too young to remain abstinent. He was a promising baseball star and every girl within fifty miles radius wanted a piece of him.

On the night of December 31st, on their assumed 18th birthday, they went to the movie as they always did each New Year's Eve, and a chance for him to kiss and finger her just a little . . . no penetration allowed. She had mastered the art of jerking him off too. It was an easy task for Pat to please him since he was known to ejaculate before Pat could spell S A M S O N three times. Condom was not in vogue then, at least, not among the cheerleading team of Sugarcaine. The male members of the team didn't give a damn . . .

On that beautiful day which turned out to be her worst nightmare, they drove to the nearby park close to the movie theater. She parked his 1992 Toyota Corolla and kissed tenderly as lovers do. Then, out of nowhere, Ted said, "Boobsy, we are eighteen now and can I have some coochy at least to celebrate? I know you don't want to have sex before marriage but I've waited for four years and I'm about sick of it. I could've any fucking girls I want but I refuse to do so, except the one time I told you about."

Pat, outraged, got up from the Toyota Corolla's back breaking stick-shift, sticking to her midrib. She buttoned up her blouse, and said, "I'm giving you nothing, stupid. If you have to sleep with those whores you threw in my face, then, best of luck to you, mother-fucker."

She opened the door and was about to walk away when Samson pulled her back into the car and said, "Bitch, get your fucking ass over here."

Crying and hysterical, she begged him to stop." Ted, think about what you're about to do. I don't want it this way. I love you . . . no, no, no. Please, Jesus, help me. No Sammy . . . please, stop it . . ."

She ran out of the park, half naked, to a nearby Jamaican convenience food store owned by a family of Indian immigrants. They assisted her to dial 911, after she claimed rape. While waiting for the authority, she replayed in her mind the verses taught to her in one of her Sunday school bible readings:

Luke 20:1-8:

> *One day Jesus was in the temple area. He was teaching the people. Jesus told the people the good news about the kingdom of God. The leading priests, teachers of the law, and older Jewish leaders came to talk to Jesus.*
>
> *They said, "Tell us! What authority do you have to do these things? Who gave you this authority?"*
>
> *Jesus answered, "I will ask you a question too. Tell me: When John baptized people, did that come from God or was it only from other people?"*
>
> *The priests, the teachers of the law, and the Jewish leaders all talked about this. They said to each other, "If we answer, 'John's baptism was from God,' then he will say, 'then why did you not believe John?' But if we say that John's baptism was from someone else, {not God,} then all the people will kill us with rocks. They*

*will kill us because they believe that John was
a prophet.*

*So they answered, "We don't know the
answer." So Jesus said to them, "Then I will
not tell you what authority I use to do these
things!"*

Pat then paraphrased the words of Jesus Christ, her Lord,
who should've protected her at this time of hurt and
disappointment, and said with tears, "By whose authority did
Ted do what he did."

She blamed herself for all that happened. She couldn't
look her parents in the eyes when they arrived. She now
considered herself not fit to be their innocent daughter. Her
life would never be the same again.

According to her narrative to the police, Ted was determined
to rape her if she refused to have consented sex with him . . ."
Officer, he was stronger. I have no chance with my 115
pounds frame to get him off me," she told the female officer
with the sympathetic ears.

"He took off my panties and forced himself on me," she told
the male officer who seemed to adore her beauty.

Ted was arrested that early morning within hours, at Pat
sister's house where he was hiding. He confessed and
apologized profusely to Pat, her parents, the officers that
arrested him, and to the whole world. He was disoriented,
tired, and just wanted to go home to his mama.

Pat went home, took hot showers which lasted for hours and
later stayed in the tub to cleanse all perceived foreign objects
from her pure body and soul.

Pat's parents quickly retained the services of the best lawyers out of town (to avoid local influences), and to make sure Ted never lived another day to do the same heinous crime against any female on the face of the planet.

Ted was arraigned the following day.

Pat's mother, Cecily Suckleford, intended to ask for the death penalty. After all, they were residents of the great state of Texas. But her husband persuaded her to reconsider such an extreme measure; considering she is a high ranking member of Texas' Organization against Death Penalty (TOAD). He pleaded with her to reconsider her resolve. "I'm equally hurting, my love," he told her.

He reminded her of the Bible passages from the gospel according to Matthews Chapter 18 on sins and forgiveness

Cecily angrily replied "Well, if that was the case, maybe, I need to stop reading the Bible or stop going to the damn church." Cecily's faith was tested. Faith has its limitation. She failed the faith test. She was only mortal. She loved her daughter, as such; rationalization was a rare commodity at that moment in her life.

Pat's parents were shocked when their attorneys directed them to the juvenile domestic court the following morning. Main reason: Ted was a juvenile. He was only 17 years, eleven months, 23 hours, and 51 minutes old on December 31, according to his birth certificate. The rape occurred at 11:51 on December 31st.

Considering all the facts and circumstances, Ted was tried as a juvenile, sentenced to reformed school, underwent ten hours of psychiatric evaluations, and was required to perform seventy five hours of community service.

Even, in the great state of Texas, there was selective injustice for "Black folk," Cecily lamented.

Pat and her parents were devastated and thereafter moved their entire family to Mississippi, to start life all over. In Mississippi, the birth place of Cecily, they felt at home. "It was the power of prayer that had walked Pat through life," her parents told her therapists.

Pat's life story may soon be an open book for all to read. In a way, she had overcome. She was encouraged to go public with her story and become a spokesperson for teenagers who had been date raped.

After twenty years of nightmares and therapy, she was ready to talk about it. Her therapists had told her many times, "Pat, you need to write a book about your experiences and let other young women near and far learn from your tragedy."

"I would do whatever it takes to put closure to my nightmares and misery," she would respond to her numerous therapists.

This was the first time Pat's husband learned of his wife's rape. The sad essence of his marriage was coming to focus.

CHAPTER 10

Pat did her best to avoid Sheila since February 5, subsequent to Ted's arrest. After two weeks, and Sheila's countless phone calls, letters, flowers, and cards, they were able to arrange a meeting at their usual café to catch up on matters of interest. Pat wanted to be distant. Sheila felt differently.

Sheila: Are you ok, Pat? You look worried and unaffectionate.

Pat: Sheila, I've come to talk to you face to face. I don't think it would be a good idea to see each other anymore, at least, not in the foreseeable future. Considering the case at hand, my attorneys have advised me to contact you and your family as little as possible or not at all.

Sheila: Could we at least see each other periodically? I want you. I need you. I'm so miserable without you. I am losing weight . . .

Pat: I don't think so, Sheila. I'm sorry.

Sheila: Are you saying you will not see me anytime soon or not at all?

Pat: Yes to both questions. That's exactly what I'm saying. I told you before we got together that it would only be for one time to celebrate my fifteenth wedding anniversary, and you agreed.

Sheila: I know you're not speaking from your heart right now, Pat. I saw the sparkles in your eyes and the way you felt me when we made love. I saw the ways I made you cum for the first time in years. I know you wanted me too. Please, don't do this to us at this time. Don't do this to me. I need you and I cannot make it without you. You're all I got now. You know it.

Pat: I need to go. Please, take care of yourself, Sheila.

Sheila: Don't leave, Pat. Don't leave me (she started to cry within the distance of other diners)

Pat: Stop being a cry baby. (She beckoned to the server for their lunch ticket)

Sheila: Fuck you, Pat. You'll regret this day.

Sheila stormed out of the café and waited in her car at the parking lot, sobbing until she saw Pat drive away. She drove behind her and called her cell number more than ten times to apologize but she could only leave messages. Déjà Vu.

After a couple of miles driving behind her, Sheila changed direction and drove home. Getting home, she went straight to the liquor cabinet for double shots of Remy Martin (VSOP). That was her first for a long time. Ordinarily, red wine was her beverage of choice, mostly at dinner or while watching Dream Girls or Ellen Show.

Her daughter, Brenda, who had changed schools and moved back home to be closer to home and support her mother asked, "Mommy, are you ok?

"I'm fine, Brenda. I just have too many sticks in the fire right now."

"I'm sorry mom; all will be fine, and good night." Her daughter replied with a kiss and a hug.

Sheila couldn't sleep. She wanted to reevaluate her strategy and accelerate how to make Pat see things her way. The stage was now set for Sheila's best performances.

--------●--------

At 2:00 am, Sheila called Pat with her daughter's cell phone. She knew Pat had blocked her number. Pat answered, "Hello." "It's me Pat. I just want to talk with you for a sec."

"Sheila, it's two in the morning. You're unfair and inconsiderate, to say the least. If you don't stop this nonsense, I'll have no choice but to . . ."

Before Pat could complete her sentence, Sheila interrupted and said, "No choice but to do what? Lock me up too as you did my husband?" True love had beclouded her judgment. She didn't even have much of a husband to speak of.

Pat hissed into the phone and hung up. "Psycho bitch," she said and tried to go back to sleep.

Paul left alone what he overheard on the phone between Pat and the presumed caller, Sheila. He wouldn't be objective in the matter even if he wanted to intervene. "There is trouble in paradise," he said aside. He loved the ways everything was developing between his two girls, as he referred to them now.

"What was bad for Pat will be bumper crop for me," he told himself.

That was his plan and hope since February 5. He had prayed about it. It seemed God was listening to his prayers and his request was still under consideration.

One week later, Sheila personally delivered to Pat's residence a bouquet of flowers with a ten-page, double spaced typed written letter. The tone of the letter was surreal, respectful, loving, apologetic, emotional, and personal.

That same day, on Tuesday afternoon, a certified letter was sent to Sheila from the law firm of Genesis and Revelations, & Co, PLLC, demanding her to cease and desist from contacting Pat in any form or shape.

"One road closed temporarily," Sheila said with a nonchalant attitude. She had planned and anticipated Pat's reaction. This time around, Pat had also messed with the wrong woman.

Sheila immediately had a change of strategy and put her plan B into action. She dialed Paul's number. His number was always available to her anytime of the day. On the second ring, she hung up to clear her thoughts. Paul immediately called her back but could only leave a message.

Paul had been calling Sheila each morning, at exactly seven thirty-five, as she had instructed him to do three weeks after

February 5. Pat leaves home for work, Monday through Saturday, at seven-thirty.

Sheila waited until that evening, to return Paul's call. He answered on first ring and immediately walked to the balcony to avoid Pat listening to his conversation.

The picture on Paul's iPhone when Sheila called was that of his project manager, Antonio Lopapez. Her number was also coded. Although, Paul might be a small time rookie of a player, he was determined to be careful and planned ahead.

Paul: Hey you. Good evening. What can I do you for yah . . . ?

Sheila: Sweetie, why don't you come over and massage my soft breasts tonight? The body-oil is ready and waiting for you at room temperature, as I like it.

Paul: Not a good idea tonight and you know that.

Sheila: Are you scared of your wife or you don't want me anymore since last Wednesday afternoon? You promised to be ready whenever I call . . .

Paul: It's just not a good idea tonight. It was your fault. Why the hell did you have to bring the flowers to my house? I asked you not to do such a thing last Wednesday . . .

Sheila: What are you wearing? What are you doing? Is your dick hard?

Paul: Excuse me?

Sheila: I just want to know, Puky.

Paul: I'm wearing my jogging suit. Pat is taking a nap. I'm relaxing and watching the first episode of American Idol, on DVD. Yes, my dick is hard now that I'm . . .

Sheila: I've better alternatives for you, Puky.

Paul: What might that be Brother Lopa?

Sheila: I guess I'm Brother Lopa, hum? The bitch is beside you . . . Why don't you put on my panties I left behind?

Paul: Excuse me?

Sheila: You hear me. I saw you when you stuck it under the mattress, the last time I was in y'all home.

Paul: What do you want from me?

Sheila: I want you to put on the panties and come over. Come and give me a bath and a massage. Like I said, the massage oil is warm and waiting. Don't forget to bring me my favorite strawberry yogurt. Maybe I may let you fuck your wife's pussy this time. If you can't obey me, as agreed, you better kiss this clean and pussy goodbye. I'll leave the front door open.

Paul: What about your daughter?

Sheila: I've taken care of my end. Come and take care of me. I don't give a shit about your end . . .

Paul: Lopa, Lopa, Lopa, Brother Lopa . . . these damn drop calls.

No response . . . the line had gone dead before Paul could convince Shelia that it might not be a good and safe night for him to leave home.

He had a choice not to go to Sheila but he wanted to go nonetheless. He had been alive from within since their encounters.

Paul quickly dressed and informed Pat that he had to run to Tight & Fresh Market to pick up a shaving cream for the following day. "Do you want anything dear," he asked his wife.

"Thanks babe, I'm alright."

Paul had been to Sheila's house a couple of times according to his version of events. The last time was the previous Wednesday for an afternoon delight. Even then, Sheila refused to "Give up the smoothie." Sheila was mainly messing with his mind. He knew that much. The state of her mind didn't matter to him anymore. He believed time and patience were on his side, however.

Paul wanted her for himself too. He was caught in the web of lust and sexual deviance he so much wanted and desired. He had appealed to Sheila countless times within the short period they had known each other that he'd pay any price to win her love. He was playing with fire. He had tasted the forbidden desire he found in her and now wanted more of it, regardless of the consequences. His life was no longer his own. He was getting weak by the minute, at every thought of her.

"These men that came into my life just don't get it," Sheila said aloud as she waited for Paul. She knew he will show up.

His soul belonged to her. Her body parts had influenced his main body part, to say the least.

The affairs have become a triangle of lust. "Sheila was at the apex; Paul and Pat were at the X axes. One axis was fighting for better positioning and the other was pretending to avoid reality.

By the time Paul arrived, Sheila was on her back, lying on her striped grey cotton sheet, half naked. She spread her legs like an eagle with pussy aroma circulating the room. The scented candles all over her room also added more allure to the occasion. She was good like that.

Paul arrived as expected like a devoted puppy coming home for dinner.

"Paul, this is what I want . . . lick her pussy as I taught you." He obeyed. Not perfect but Sheila agreed that Paul had improved his performances since his anniversary night.

"I thought you wanted me to give you a bath, a massage, and . . . ?" Paul asked. He was truly in love. Yes, love comes easily for him, considering the stale sex with his wife.

"You're here or do you want to go back home to that stupid wife of yours?" she sultrily said. She was really good at her craft. They both ignored the strawberry and caramel on a china plate on the table . . .

Paul dipped a red juicy strawberry into the caramel and offered it to Sheila. She rejected his love gesture with a thank you. He ate it instead. As he was sitting at the edge of the bed getting ready to leave from unfulfilled booty call, Sheila switched on the play button on her DVD with a remote control besides her bed. The twenty nine minutes homemade documentary that appeared on her 72 inch plasma TV was all about the pussy licking that just transpired between her and Paul.

Paul was shocked and equally elated about his performances on digital. He was tall, handsome, with a smooth skin. He looked clean-shaven, athletic, and for a forty something years old, he knew his sexual prowess was exemplary. It was his first sexual act on video. He wished Pat had had the wisdom to do the same. He ate more strawberries as he continued to watch his pussy-licking on display . . .

Unfortunately, he was so whipped by Sheila's pussy and his resolve to have her exclusively like the men before him, that he forgot that his action and the digital recording of the evening's episode may come back to haunt him. Mortal men always repeat past mistakes. He wasn't an exception. Since he has no future career in politics, he really didn't care, whatever Sheila has on digital, unless . . .

Even in 2012, if he had taken the time to read George Orwell's 1984, *Big Brother,* or if he had been watching *Maury* or *Cheaters* on primetime for some guidance, he would've realized that anything private by the constitution is now considered public by the same government that is setup to protect it. In his current state of mind, however, he didn't give a damn about the consequences of his actions.

"Paul, you can have your copy of the CD if you like. If you do, keep it in a safe place before your sorry-ass wife sees it. This is between us and for you to watch at your leisure when you miss me. I know you will. I'll also review the tape later to see where you'll need improvements, the next time I call you for full service. You know I can't contact your wife right now, so, you have a temporary reprieve to contact me anytime, directly. Here is my private cell number you had been demanding. This is your lucky moment. Obey me and you'll be fine."

Although Paul was stunned, confused, and speechless, he cared less.

Sheila then stood, put on her push up bra, placed one of her legs on the coffee table, with her pussy at an angle said, "I'll see you tomorrow. But first, hear this, pussy cat:

> From now on, I'll only let you fuck me when I think you deserve it.
>
> You can no longer fuck your wife if you want to taste me again.
>
> I know you want more of me. If you behave, I may let you have my red rose when I think you deserve it.
>
> FYI, Ted, I mean Paul, the tape is one of my calling cards. Make a note of it and don't disobey me. It will not be pretty, if you piss me off.
>
> One last thing Puky my dear, let me remind you of an adage: Use people, who have something to gain, not people with nothing to lose. I have nothing to lose Paul.
>
> Get it? At this point, you have a lot to lose. So be afraid, and don't mess with me.
>
> Ok, lover boy, enjoy the tape and see you at 6:30 tomorrow. I won't call to remind you again. Don't be late and don't let the door hit you on your way out.
>
> Oh, lest I forgot, don't forget to bring me Pat's pink panties you said she wore to work today as promised.

Paul, you may need to start writing these things down since you seem to forget my requests lately. You must be juggling too many of us . . .

On his way home, Paul recounted the life he had shared with his wife Pat, to-date. He had many joyous moments and some sad times. His marriage, even by the loosest definition, wasn't all that bad. In his mind, however, he knew the passion, affection, and love they once shared would never be the same. Paul was now a divided man. He wanted to love and stay with his wife but never understood why the vacuum was widening so fast between them. More importantly, he never understood the reason his wife kept from him the rape episode that affected her so much. He never understood why his wife's career always came first in their marriage.

He never understood the reason his wife only wanted to conceive through the Almighty's blessing alone and at the same time was taking birth control pills she kept hidden in her coat pocket in her closet. At the same time, she kept another full set of birth control pills by the bed stand to convince him that she wasn't on the pill.

He never understood the reason Sheila turned his wife on so much on February 5, the day that finally made it clear that his wife who had denied, like the plaque, her disdain to be with any women countless times, may be at a minimum, bi-curious.

In the final analysis, Sheila was just a catalyst to a marriage that had ended the day it started. Sheila was a mean to an end, certainly to his marriage that will soon come to an end whether he wanted it or not. He prayed to God and wished his thoughts were wrong.

Paul then recounted the synopsis of Pat's life to-date:

Pat was highly educated, intelligent, tall, hour glass shape, proportional, and very attractive. Actress Grace Kelly in her younger years came to mind when he spoke about Pat's beauty. They had been marriage for fifteen years. No children. She had her undergraduate degree in mathematics, a master's degree in public administration, a JD, and was a graduate of the police academy. She was once the chief of staff for the mayor of OldPort before her current position as the acting chief of police for the city of Kope. It was rumored that her current appointment was a political reward for her silence after she caught a married city official in an uncompromising position with a 20-year old undocumented Mexican nanny in his SUV, in the city's park. The official who had since separated from his wife as a result of his sexual sloppiness was a contender in the gubernatorial race. Pat's testimony was crucial to his campaign and possibly his divorce.

Thereafter, Pat became a star and a political darling when she reversed her original statement and denied, under oath, that she never saw the city official in the park on the day in question or anywhere else for that matter. That was her story. She stuck to it under oath. So much for testifying under oath . . .

She was asked by the prosecutor, "Ms. Peterman, did you see his Hon. with his pants down?"

"No sir, I saw him the same time I saw you zipping up your own pant, Mr. Prosecutor," she emphatically answered. The part of her testimony about the prosecutor was true.

"Objection, your Honor. Could I treat Ms. Peterman as a hostile witness?" the prosecutor fired back.

"Ok, I guess," the judge said. The rest was history.

All charges against her future governor were later dropped without comments. No one will ever know what transpired in the city park that day in question. Power corrupts and beauty corrupts absolutely.

However, since being in office, Pat's subordinates admired and respected her. The city council that appointed her was exonerated of their alleged "Preferential employment," because of her brilliant performances on the job—within eight months of assuming office, crime rate in the city of OldPort had gone down eight percent and race relations had improved four percentage points.

She was a regular on local and statewide TV, speaking on issues affecting female youths and teenage pregnancy. Her crusade also addressed the high rate of high school dropouts among her race. Her achievements overall were very impressive.

She was the first African American to hold her current position in the city's 123-year history. Many had asked her to consider running for statewide office one day and soon. She had played around with the idea but considering the current political environment, she was having second thoughts . . .

A former black owned MFTV, now a subsidiary of a British based media conglomerate, wanted to interview her once but later cancelled her TV appearance for unspecified reasons. It was rumored that her testimony and political affiliation with the future governor might be the reason. Hoxy news might come calling instead . . .

CHAPTER 11

The two opposing lawyers filed the legal briefs to the court on behalf of Patricia Peterman, (plaintiff) and Theodore Samson, (defense) for the mayhem that occurred at Pat's residence on February 5.

In their opening statements, the lawyers for the defense wanted Pat to dismiss the remaining charges against their client, Ted, because they believed the charges were bogus, unfounded, baseless, misuse and abuse of political power, and without merits. They also urged the plaintiff, to allow wisdom and common sense to prevail. As such, she should let the "Sleeping dog lie."

They further pleaded with Pat's legal team that no one would benefit at the end of the day except the financial windfall to the lawyers representing both parties. They also concluded that the lives of both parties may never be the same again—an unusual admission by trial lawyers.

Instead, the lawyers for the plaintiff, at the insistence of their client, Pat, refused to negotiate. Pat will always be Pat. Her way was the only way. She wanted revenge at all cost. She was determined to win, as she had done in her life, in all her endeavors. She wanted to finally get even with Theodore Samson, the rapist.

Sadly, Pat had set the stage for a failed war. Her battle that started twenty something years ago was now fully engaged. This was her last stand. This was her war and she intended to win it.

A deposition testimony was conducted in the defense's 100-member law firm. Pat's lead Attorney, Osaro Egharevba, Esq. (attorney for the plaintiff) conducted the deposition.

Mr. Theodore Samson was deposed first.

Pa wanted to be excused from the room when Ted, the defendant, was being deposed because she didn't want to be in the same room with him. She was advised to stay.

Attorney:	Could you give your full name, address, and occupation for the record, please?
Ted:	My name is Theodore Samson. I have no permanent residence at the moment because the property allocated to me, as part of my separation agreement, was damaged by flood. I have no flood insurance. I'm now staying at the shelter. I had also lost my job since the arrest incident with my employer, a federal security defense contractor doing brisk business in Afghanistan.
Attorney:	Where then is your shelter address?
Ted:	5555 Innocent Lane . . .
Attorney:	Were you in the plaintiff's residence on the evening of February 5, 2012?
Ted:	Yes sir.

Attorney: Did you enter Chief Patricia Peterman's residence on the day in question?

Ted: No sir. I only knocked at her front door.

Attorney: Why was that?

Ted: To talk to my wife and take her home to celebrate her birthday.

Attorney: Were you invited?

Ted: No sir.

Attorney: How did you know your wife was at attorney Peterman's house?

Ted: I drove around for hours looking for her.

Attorney: You're under oath. How did you know exactly your wife was at Ms. Peterman's residence?

Ted: Like I said, I received a phone call, drove around, and saw my wife's car in front of their house.

Attorney: Did you say you received a phone call? When, about what, and from who?

Ted: Never mind. I don't remember.

Attorney: Had you ever been to the plaintiff's house before that evening?

Ted: No sir.

Attorney: So you just happen to wonder to the plaintiff residence after driving around a city of over 400,000 single family homes?

Ted: Yeah. I mean, yes.

Attorney: How did you know the house belong to the plaintiff again?

Ted: She is the chief of police and everybody . . .

Attorney: Were you stalking her?

Ted: Heck no. She wished.

Attorney: Watch your language, please. Have you met Ms. Peterman before?

Ted: No sir.

Attorney: You're still under oath. Are you sure of that?

Ted: I thought you meant earlier that day. Yes, we had met before.

Attorney: Had Ms. Peterman ever been a guest in your house?

Ted: I didn't invite her. I never invited her to my home.

Attorney: That was not what I asked you Mr. Samson. Please, answer my question.

Ted: Yes sir. She was an uninvited guest in my house a couple of times.

Attorney:	Have you known Ms. Peterman intimately before you met her in your residence?
Ted:	Ummm . . .
Attorney:	I can't hear you, sir.
Ted:	Maybe
Attorney:	How?
Ted:	We dated briefly.
Attorney:	Would it be accurate to say you dated for about four years?
Ted:	You can say that.
Attorney:	I just said that. We want your own answer, sir.
Ted:	Maybe.
Attorney:	That was when you raped her?
Ted:	Those charges were dropped and expunged from my records. I was a minor then, in case you want to be reminded Mr. big shot attorney.
Attorney:	Ok then, Mr. Samson, were you under the influence of alcohol and/or illegal drugs when you attacked Ms. Peterman's house?
Ted:	No. I didn't attack her house. I only knocked.
Attorney:	Were you armed and/or in possession of narcotics? Remember, you're under oath.

Ted: The cops planted the drugs on me. They have no proof.

Attorney: They planted it on you or they have no proof it belongs to you. Which was it?

Ted: It was not mine. They have no proof either.

Attorney: What was the knife the cops found in your car glove compartment for?

Ted: Did they have a search warrant to go through my stuff?

Attorney: We ask the question and you answer it, Mr. Samson. For your information, they had probable cause . . .

Ted: It's mine.

Attorney: We already established that. Why did you bring it to Ms. Peterman's house?

Ted: I always have it for my own protection in case . . .

Attorney: So you came armed to stab Ms. Peterman, in case she refused to cooperate?

Ted: Hell fucking no.

Attorney: Ok then. Were you jealous of your wife's status in the community? Were you jealous of her because she was in a better circle of friends and made more money than you do?

Ted: Are you kidding me? I thought we are here to talk about my wife fucking Patricia and her husband?

Attorney: You have no evidence of that, Mr. Samson.

Ted: Not when she opened the door wearing practically nothing.

Attorney: Who had practically nothing on?

Ted: Boobsy

Attorney: Who?

Ted: Excuse me, Ms. Patricia Peterman.

Attorney: Did you see the plaintiff and your wife kissing or having sex?

Ted: No. But what do you think they were doing naked all over the place?

Attorney: Once again, I'm the one asking the question, here. Did you see them together? Yes or no, Mr. Samson, please.

Ted: What do you mean?

Attorney: Fine. Do you see your wife making love to Ms. Peterman?

Ted: No, I didn't.

Attorney: Were you mad because you weren't invited to their party?

Ted: Excuse me? What party?

Attorney: Did you actually see your wife in the plaintiff's residence?

Ted: No sir, but . . .

Attorney: When was the last time you spoke with your wife as a loving couple?

Ted: Maybe about twenty one days ago. I'm not counting.

Attorney: Why do you think your wife refused to be present and testify for you here today?

Ted: I don't know Mr. Attorney. You tell me . . .

Attorney: Yes, I will. Could it be because you had abused her and she is afraid of you?

Ted: I never laid my hands on my wife or children. God is my witness.

Attorney: Did you ever see your wife sleeping with Ms. Peterman in your house? You are under oath, Mr. Samson

Ted: No, but I'm sure she did.

Attorney: When was the last time you made love to your lovely wife?

Ted: That is a private matter.

Attorney:	No longer private sir. Not when you accused the plaintiff of having sex with your wife. Please, answer the question.
Ted:	I can't remember. She no longer wanted to fuck me, if that's what you meant.
Attorney:	Please, mind your language again. Who is Mr. Busybody?
Ted:	He is my fraternity brother. He has been helping me out during my trying time. Life hadn't been easy for me lately if you care to know . . .
Attorney:	Did you discuss the allegations with him?
Ted:	I don't know what you're talking about.
Attorney:	You were under a gag order not to discuss the case with anyone.
Ted:	We were just hanging out, drinking, smoking or something like that. Maybe I did.
Attorney:	Were you smoking marijuana when you discussed the case with him? I remind you again that you're under oath.
Ted:	I only smoke Marlboro light, sir. Smoking weed would be violating my parole.
Attorney:	Are you willing to take a drug, hair follicle, and a lie detector tests?

Ted: Of course not, counsel. You know lie detector test isn't admissible in court.

Attorney: You are now an attorney, hum. Who are Juliet La'Dickson and Zu Cho Samson?

Ted: Why are you bringing them into this? What have they got to do with the case?

Attorney: Again, I ask the questions, sir. Please, answer my question. May I remind you, you're still under oath?

Ted: Juliet was my lady friend and Zu is my daughter living in Bangkok with her mother.

Attorney: By lady friend, you meant girlfriend?

Ted: Correct.

Attorney: How long has that relationship been going on during your marriage?

Ted: About seven years now.

Attorney: Are you still having an affair with her?

Ted: As a matter of fact, she had nothing to do with me anymore for the last four months since I refused to leave my wife and children for her. I think she got a new lover, a mama's boy, for that matter and . . .

Attorney: Did your wife know about these other people in your life?

Ted: May be not.

Attorney: Why may that be?

Ted: That's my damned business, Mr. Attorney.

Attorney: So you have been living a double life and lying about it as you are doing now?

Ted: My private life isn't the issue here and that's all I would say about that.

Attorney: Mr. Samson, I'm getting fed up with your lies and deceits. As I see it, you're a failure to yourself, your family, and your parents, to say the least. You have no job or place to lay your head. You lied to your own wife and family and hid from them all your affairs and illegitimate children all over the globe: South Korea, Bangkok, and good heavens, anywhere else in South East Asia. Let us not forget to mention your accumulation of concubines as if you're King Solomon. God only knew how many of those. You were intoxicated, armed, and high on drugs when you attacked Ms. Peterman's house on February 5th, thinking you could assault and rape her again as you did in your house several times, or as you did in your car years ago. Or maybe, you were there to rape and stab her again thinking she was home alone. You said you were looking for your wife. What wife, Mr. Samson? A woman you hardly spoke to for God only knew when. A wife you hardly made love to anymore. But now, all of a sudden, you were concerned about her welfare or where she went. You came to the plaintiff's peaceful home drunk and under the influence of illegal substances to look for a wife who might not have been at their residence . . .

Ted: But my wife's car was parked outside their house.

Attorney: Ok then. What are your wife's car license plate number, color, and model?

Ted: Her plate number is SHELICKS. It was a red BMW coupe.

Attorney: Did you know the plaintiff has a similar car, color, and model with a license plate number CITICHE?

Ted: I don't know that.

Attorney: Are you still sure you saw your wife's car that day?

Ted: Hum . . . I thought so.

Attorney: Of course not, Mr. Samson. You were high on illegal substance and delusional . . .

Ted: I know she was there. I just knew it with my gut feeling.

Attorney: Gut feeling is not enough. Did you talk to your wife in the plaintiff's residence?

Ted: Boobsy, I mean Patricia, told me my wife was there and didn't want to talk to me.

Attorney: Are you sure? Remember, you were loaded
               with alcohol and . . .

Ted: She told me so and . . .

Attorney: Are you still in love with Mrs. Peterman,
               your rape victim, you casually and constantly
               referred to as "Boobsy?"

Ted: Hell no. Fuck the bitch . . .

At this juncture, Mr. Samson had had enough. He stood up
and interrupted the plaintiff's lawyers while ranting like the
comedian, Michael Richards' racist tirade at an L.A comedy
club.

He stormed out of the room and gave the middle finger to the
plaintiff's legal team . . . "Fuck y'all son of bitches."

The plaintiff's leading lawyer, Osaro, commented, "That
fellow has psychological issues. He needs to be committed."

All parties agreed to an hour lunch break.

It would be Mrs. Patricia Peterman's turn to face the music.

———————————————•◉•———————————————

The deposition testimony of Patricia Peterman was brutal
and unfriendly by a team of attorneys determined to make
names for themselves and their law firm, headquartered on
K Street in Washington DC. The firm was the same law firm
that represented Ted during his rape charges twenty or so
years ago. They also did brisk business lobbying for many
countries in Africa, South East Asia, and Central America.

Ted exercised his rights, and returned to the room to face
his accuser, acting chief, Patricia Peterman. He wanted to be
close to the lady he used to call Boobsy and would've once
died for. After all, he had once given her the best four years
of his youth too. He was really in love with her then and . . .

Mrs. Peterman was sworn in and promised to tell the truth
and nothing but the truth.

Ted's lead attorney, Jerome Jesus Cummings, Jr. (JJC), was
ready to destroy Pat once and fall all.

Attorney:	Good afternoon, Chief Peterman. How are you doing today?
Patricia:	Good afternoon everyone. I'm doing fine, sir. One point of correction, I'm not a Chief. I'm only acting chief. Thank you.
Attorney:	Ok. Thanks for the information. Could you give us your name, address, and occupation for the record, please?
Patricia:	My name is attorney Patricia Peterman. I lived at ABC Circle, OldPort (Public policy doesn't allow disclosure of the addresses of top government officials). I'm acting police chief in the city of Kope.
Attorney:	How did you come to know Mr. Samson, the defendant?
Patricia:	We met over 20 years ago at Victory High and we dated for nearly four years before he raped me.

Attorney:	Excuse me, that rape charges had been dismissed. Ms. Patricia, what were you doing in the house of the person you accused of raping you, on the afternoon of January 11th?
Patricia:	I went to visit my sorority sister, who I later found out to be his wife.
Attorney:	So you made it your duty to visit the wife of the person you accused of all sorts of unfounded allegations, including rape?
Patricia:	I didn't know they were husband and wife at the time I went there. I went there to discuss sorority matters.
Attorney:	Chief, you're still under oath. Are you sure that was the only reason?
Patricia:	I know I'm under oath counselor. I don't need to be reminded in every question.
Attorney:	Answer the question, please.
Patricia:	That's my answer.
Attorney:	Did you remember what you discussed at this supposed private sorority meeting?
Patricia:	We discussed a lot of things including the weather.
Attorney:	My question is not funny at all, Chief Peterman.

Patricia: We discussed sorority matters and our college days.

Attorney: Was that before or after you were caught in bed with her?

Patricia: Excuse me? What bed? I briefly fell asleep on her couch.

Attorney: And naked too?

Patricia: Excuse me?

Attorney: Please, answer the question.

Patricia: I wasn't naked.

Attorney: Why then were you covered by her blanket? Why were you naked under the cover? Why were your article of clothing folded neatly somewhere else in her house?

Patricia: I wasn't naked.

Attorney: Why were your blouse and pants folded neatly over her loveseat, Chief?

Patricia: I didn't want to ruffle them.

Attorney: Yah . . .

Patricia: That was the truth.

Attorney: Including your panties hung over her bed post and one of your shoes in the den and the other in her daughter's bedroom?

Patricia:	I don't know what you are talking about. My clothes were stained. Maybe I made a mistake coming to her house that day.
Attorney:	Stained with what, chief? What about your shoes all over her house?
Patricia:	Why are you trying to make everything dirty?
Attorney:	Chief, you're under oath. Were you and the defendant's wife an item?
Patricia:	What do you mean? We are friends, if that's what you meant.
Attorney:	Did you ever leave any of your personal belongings at the defendant's house?
Patricia:	No sir.
Attorney:	Did you remember texting the defendant's wife to keep an item of yours?
Patricia:	I can't recollect.
Attorney:	Chief, let me joggle your memory then. Here is a copy of a text from you to our client's wife, and I quote, "Keep the panties sweetie as a reminder of our meeting."
Patricia:	If my memory serves me well, that text was meant for my husband when we were role playing after one of our monthly rendezvous at a local hotel to inject fire into our marriage.

Attorney: Is your marriage in trouble? Please, don't
               answer that. Chief, did you know our client's
               wife told her husband, and I quote, "Pat will
               be mine if she would have me."

Patricia: That's hearsay. She isn't here. How can I
               challenge what she said to her husband?

Attorney: We ask the questions, please.

Patricia: Fine. I don't know anything about that.

Attorney: We also have here multitude e-mails from
               you to our client's wife. Were you having an
               affair with her? Did you promise her you will
               leave your husband for her? Did you set up all
               those lunch dates with her? Who paid for the
               lunches? Why did you buy her all those gifts
               from Victoria's secret?

Patricia: You want me to answer all these questions
               now or you want a book report? I plead the 5th
               and . . . what Victoria's secret?

Attorney: Alright then. Did you know Sheila is bisexual?
               You're still under oath.

Patricia: I'm aware of that counselor. In fact, I knew she
               is a lesbian.

Attorney: Did you celebrate any special occasion
               recently?

Patricia: Yes, my fifteenth year wedding anniversary?

Attorney: Where, Chief Peterman?

Patricia: In my house.

Attorney: For such a special occasion, how many friends and family members did you invite to celebrate your anniversary with you?

Patricia: None. I wanted it to be private and special between me and my husband.

Attorney: I cherish privacy myself, Ms. Peterman. If I heard you correctly, you celebrated the occasion with your husband alone?

Patricia: Yes.

Attorney: Do you have a housemaid?

Patricia: Yes, sir. We are proud of her.

Attorney: That's commendable. What's her name again?

Patricia: Angelika.

Attorney: Was she present at your anniversary celebration?

Patricia: Of course not.

Attorney: Are you sure of that?

Patricia: Aaaa . . .

Attorney: Ok, Mrs. Peterman. We will get back to that later as well.

Patricia: Fine . . .

Attorney: What day did you celebrate this so called special occasion?

Patricia: I can't recollect . . .

Attorney: You could not recollect the day of your anniversary, Ms. Patricia?

Patricia: As I said, I couldn't recollect.

Attorney: Ok then. Had Mrs. Samson ever visited your house?

Patricia: May be.

Attorney: What date was that maybe, please?

Patricia: I can't recollect.

Attorney: Does February 5th sound about right?

Patricia: If you said so.

Attorney: Chief, I just said so. Answer my question, please?

Patricia: Yes.

Attorney: So, your so called private celebration was not between you and your husband alone after all?

Patricia: Aaaa . . .

Attorney: We have a witness and affidavit that . . .

Patricia: She stopped by only to give me a gift.

Attorney: So, you weren't alone all night, on the day of your anniversary celebration?

Patricia: I guess so now, if you put it that way. No. She didn't spend the night . . .

Attorney: Oh, why not?

Patricia: She went back home to meet her daughter . . .

Attorney: We have here public reports that your wedding anniversary was actually March 16th. So Chief, are you saying you had an early anniversary?

Patricia: Ummm . . .

Attorney: Ok, we would get back to that later too, Chief.

Patricia: We planned and pick that day to . . .

Attorney: Chief, we'll get back to that later as we said. You may need time to get your story straight. Are you bisexual, Chief? You're still under oath.

Patricia: Definitely not.

Attorney: Can you describe the gift Mrs. Samson gave you?

Patricia: That was private and personal.

Attorney: Did that gift make you walk around the house naked in the presence of your gift-giver-sorority sister, while all the lights in your house were dimmed?

Patricia: It's my house, counselor. I still have the right in this country to do what I want to do or wear what I want to wear or nothing at all, or even sleep anywhere I want in the privacy of my home.

Attorney: Was anything missing in your house recently?

Patricia: I can't think of any.

Then, one of the defense attorneys brought out a pair of pink panties from his coat pocket and asked Pat, did you recognize these?

Patricia: They are my underwear.

Attorney: How did they get into our client's house?

Patricia: How should I know?

Attorney: We ask the questions Chief. Please, answer the question.

Patricia: I don't know how they got there.

Attorney: I thought you said she was the one giving you gifts and not the other way around? You're still under oath, Chief.

Patricia: Maybe she stole it. I never gave her my underwear as gifts.

Attorney: Or you left it during your countless visits.

Patricia: I never left my panties in her house as I said earlier.

Attorney: Are you calling your so called sorority sister a thief?

Patricia: I have no clue how she got hold of my panties.

Attorney: Did you give her any other gifts then?

Patricia: I cannot recollect.

Attorney: Attorney Peterman, you don't seem to remember much lately. Well, I have to ask, have you ever left your night gown in our client's wife bed?

Patricia: No, counselor.

Attorney: Mrs. Peterman, we have text messages here that read, and I quote, "Sweetie, I forgot my nightie in your room . . . I'll pick it up next time . . . . BTW, you ought to take it off me with your teeth next time. Pink is my color . . ."

Patricia: It was just a joke.

Attorney: Are you saying you didn't leave your night gown in her room or your text messages were jokes?

Patricia: Can I see the text, please?

Attorney: Here you go.

Patricia: They are not mine.

Attorney: Is that your final answer?

Patricia: Yes counselor.

Attorney: We will get back to that later too.

Patricia: Your cup of tea, counselor.

Attorney: We also have here multitude e-mails from you. And for your information, we also have in our possession a few of your panties worn by Mrs. Samson the night of your so-called private celebration and several time thereafter. So, chief, would you be willing to provide us with one of your used panties for a DNA test?

Patricia: I didn't wear panties.

Attorney: So, you were already prepared for the orgy before your gift came to you?

Patricia: There was no orgy. There was no gift, aaah.

Attorney: Again Mrs. Peterson, would you provide us with your panties for a DNA test?

Patricia: I couldn't because I just don't put on underwear at home.

Attorney: Any old panties will do.

Patricia: I will not, pervert . . .

Attorney: Excuse me; what do you just call me?

Patricia: Never mind.

Attorney: How then do you explain this pink panty with your initial, PP on it?

Patricia: I can't explain that as I told you.

Attorney: Did you take hypnosis classes while in police academy?

Patricia: What has that got to do with this case?

Attorney: Chief, we ask the questions and you answer them. And we can ask any questions we want once your house had been turned into sexual colony that was probably illegal under the laws of a dozen states in this God blessed country.

Patricia: Yes, I did. I received an "A" too.

Attorney: Did you hypnotize Mrs. Samson the day in question?

Patricia: No. I didn't. She was in my house voluntarily.

Attorney: If she was not hypnotized, why did she have a large picture of you in her guestroom with the caption in her own hand writing, "My redeemer and savior?"

Patricia: I have no clue.

Attorney: We have here a copy of a check made payable to the police benevolent fund. Why did Mrs. Samson donate $50,000 to your city Police Community Development Project Funds on the 8th of February?

Patricia: I never knew she was the donor.

Attorney: Was the payment for services rendered or an extortion payment to drop the remaining charges against her husband?

Patricia: Excuse me?

Attorney: Did your husband, Mr. Peterman, receive the same gift or was the so-called gift only for you?

Patricia: The gift was for both of us.

Attorney: What was the gift again?

Patricia: That was private and . . .

Attorney: Right! Right!!

Patricia: It was private and that was it.

Attorney: Chief Peterman, let me ask you as straight forward as I can because I'm getting sick of your manipulations and distortions. Did that privacy and gifts include an orgy with another man's wife? Did that privacy include you seeing with the defendant's wife at several restaurants, several times in cozy positions, countless times, all over the city, in recent past? Did that privacy include both of you seen by witnesses coming out of a matinée movie in January 28th? Did that privacy include you visiting the wife of the defendant at their house (God only knew how many times) for over seven hours on January 11th to the extent you have to be kicked out by her husband when he caught you having an affair with his wife in their den? Did that privacy include observation by a member of your own police force (let me read the police reports again so that I can quote your own officer correctly), "I observed the complainer's husband, Mr. Peterman, behind the curtain, sodomizing Ms. Sheila Samson with a blue long dildo-shaped dick, curved like a boomerang, at their residence located at . . ."

Chief Peterman, we submit to you that we have records from the florists and retail stores enumerating all the gifts you gave to our client's wife. We have records of the time, locations, and many tickets for all the lunches, movie dates, and dinner dates you had with her. We have the evidence that you had affairs with her. We have documentation, testimonies, and notarized statements to support all that transpired on the night of February 5th in your abode. We have a witness familiar with your household who is more than willing to testify to all the events that occurred on that day and beyond. Practically Chief Peterman, we have documents and pictures showing that you turned your house into nothing but a brothel with our client's innocent wife to satisfy your own sexual deviance, using your political power to persuade her.

Considering all these, I ask you, could you honestly believe our client had no reason or reasons to protect his wife from your sexual tentacles? We are here today to stop you before you destroyed his happy home, corrupt his innocent and respectful wife, and turned his two lovely young children into . . .

Patricia: You're lying and badgering me sir.

Attorney: We are done here. But we reserve the right to ask you more questions, when we see fit. Don't leave town anytime soon.

Patricia: All your allegations were untrue and malicious.

Attorney: One more question Ms. Peterman. Have you being sending your husband to check on Ms. Sheila Samson every Wednesday around 7:37am since you sent a "No contact" letter from your lawyer to the defendant's wife?

Patricia: No. I didn't do such a thing.

Attorney: Would you consider withdrawing all the remaining charges against our client?

Patricia: I'll have to think about that.

Attorney: Chief, we need your answer right now.

Patricia: I have to think about it considering the new discoveries and allegations in this deposition.

Attorney: Again, we are done. However, be advised that we have no choice but to go to court and let twelve of your own peers decide the merits of these trumped up charges against our client. We believe strongly that our client is innocent. We submit to you that our client was only trying to protect and save his loving wife from kidnapping, abuse of power, secret society orgy, and brain washing. Good afternoon, Chief. Good afternoon everyone.

The case was later slated to be tried without a jury to minimize the sensation of the proceedings, considering the public image of the plaintiff, Chief Peterman.

The judge would be the final arbiter. The Judge's hearing and ruling were expected in 60 days after the deposition.

Ten days later, Pat met with her team of lawyers. She advised them that she had decided to dismiss all charges against Mr. Samson. Her lawyers concurred and informed the defendant's team of lawyers accordingly.

Pat's lawyers knew all along they had a weak case at best. Her decision was communicated to the Judge.

A copy of the judge's dismissal was sent to Ted's attorneys in earnest.

Unfortunately, the good news could not be delivered to Ted in person, at the shelter.

He had been restrained many times at the shelter, for chasing after a 26 year-old Caucasian female staff member believing she was his wife, Sheila. For all practical purposes, his love for his wife, and many other side kicks everywhere had really made him mad.

He had since been moved to a military mental hospital for psychiatrist's evaluation.

After all the allegations were dropped by Pat against Ted, the rape transcripts, summarized below, were made public as part of the agreement.

At the rape trial twenty years ago, Patricia Suckleford accused Ted of date rape.

Supported by police accounts, Ted's lawyers presented to the court the preposterous accusation which later provided the corner stone for the judge's decision to dismiss the case against him:

> *That a young lady, Ms. Patricia Suckleford who had just been raped (they quoted from the police investigators' notes), "Her hair was in place, her red lipstick, like the one Madonna wore in "Material girl," was not smeared. The buttons of her white tight top were all present. There was no stain on her matching white panties. Ted's finger print wasn't found anywhere on her private parts. His teeth marks found around her nipples were later proved not to be fresh marks.*

They further proved that she was the one that drove Ted's car to the park because according to her statement, "I know a secluded spot to make out." She was the one stroking Ted's penis because she wanted to please him and keep him away from her vagina, and other girls.

She admitted during interrogation, that she had performed the same acts on him more than a dozen times before the alleged rape.

They were able to prove that she was not a virgin, after all. There was enough evidence and a witness who would collaborate that she had slept with and had sex with her high school football linebacker, a.k.a, Pretty Face, for months before she started dating Ted. Furthermore, Ted's semen was not present in her vagina when she was tested for intercourse. Her only answer to the semen question was, "I took a long shower for two weeks after the incident to wash away the rape before going to the hospital for medical evaluation

Ted was tried as a juvenile and the case against him was later dismissed for lack of evidence. His team of lawyers, at $425 an hour, was able to prove to the satisfaction of the court, his innocence.

His lawyers earned every penny for their services. His legal fees totaled $100,655.09. Final installment was paid within ninety days after the case was dismissed.

Ms. Patricia Suckleford and her family concluded, there was no justice without money, influence, and adequate representation.

———————————•●•———————————

It was now clear the main reason attorney Patricia Peterman pursued a law degree, and a career in law enforcement. She was scorned and had a vendetta against Ted. It was for the same reason she moved to OldPort, the city where Ted had resided for the past fourteen years as a model citizen. She wanted revenge. She wanted her brand of revenge, at all cost.

———————————•●•———————————

Now that the allegations against Ted had been dropped, Patricia just wanted to turn a new page in her life and move on with her career. She wished, in silence, that she never pursued the revenge for the date rape or had him arrested to begin with.

She regretted entertaining Sheila's advances and erotic suggestions. She blamed herself for her sexual adventure to put spice in her marriage and to have suggested the threesome to her husband. At last, she admitted, to a limited extent, her failures. She was too late, however.

The lowest point in her life came on the morning of April 16, when she was told that another candidate had been appointed the permanent chief of police for the city of Kope.

She later learned from an anonymous source that the select search committee for the permanent police chief position was uncomfortable with the rumors of her past sexual escapades. The city was not ready to deal with another scandal within eight months.

However, she was a strong woman and determined to move on. She did.

CHAPTER 12

Within a couple of months, through another sorority sister, on the Pugo city council, Pat was able to secure and accept a chief of police position in one of Texas' largest cities, Warsaw.

In a way, she was going home. In a way, she needed the change of environment. In a way, she wanted to leave behind ten years of her life preoccupied with Ted, his wife, her own rocky marriage, unfulfilled career, and all the rumors she had endured in the city of Kope and environs.

After all, "City folk" talked. Talk they did, all over town, to the extent that a local folk singer wrote a song about her extracurricular activities. The song was titled: The wild side of our famed and colorful Madame in power. The song had over 81,000 hits within an hour it was posted on YouTube.

In early spring, Pat moved to the great state of Texas to resume her new appointment. She left behind her husband in their multi-million dollar mansion on the Bay. They agreed to put the house on the market. He agreed to stay behind, supervise the sale of the house, and then move down to Texas as he had done many times in support of her careers. The current downturn in the real estate market, however, might make the sale of such opulent Mansion a little harder to sell. They both knew it. He was ok with it.

They also agreed that Paul will shuttle back and forth to Warsaw every weekend. On the surface, their life seemed closer to normal again. He had always tried to accommodate his wife without expressing his opinion. To him, nothing maters because Pat will be Pat once Pat had decided what Pat wanted. This time, however, he had another incentive to stay behind other than the sale of the house no matter how long it stayed on the market . . . He had rejected, to the dismay of the realtor, two reasonable offers just to delay the sale. To him, Sheila was now part of the sale equation.

Paul was having the best of both worlds. He was able to see Sheila during the week and be with his wife on weekends. He was the luckiest man on the face of the planet especially to those who shared his new lifestyle and beliefs. He might have been an official monogamous man, but from all indications, he was living the life of a polygamist. Cool. Miraculously, Paul had just become a blessed man in America with satisfied sexual dreams without praying for it.

To his fans in the Southwest of the United States who wanted to be like him, the new arrangement would have been considered perfect. In the minds of many of his African brethren in or from the continent, his cozy state of affairs would've been celebrated as a windfall and a blessing. In a handful of African cities, streets would have been named after him.

On the other hand, he no longer had control over his future or actions. Sheila was now in full control. Shit, he was ok with that too. In his mind, he recounted, "Those without sin should cast the first stone." He was at peace with himself. Nothing else mattered.

Sheila became impatient, especially during her loneliness on weekends when Paul was away in Texas with his wife. She fine-tuned her strategy once again, as she always did when things were not going her way. She recalibrated her actions to achieve her original intent: to be with Pat.

To detached observers, Sheila has many flaws: she wanted what she wanted; when she wanted it, and as fast as she could get it, regardless of whom she crushed in the process . . . She was selfish. Frankly, she didn't give a damn. In her mind, she saw nothing wrong with her state of mind. It's obvious, Sheila and Pat, are opposite sides of the same coin.

Sheila was now moving in and out of Paul's house unchecked. Pat, the cat, was out of the house, and Sheila, the mouse, was now running free and loose in Mr. and Mrs. Peterman's Mansion on the Bay.

She was now having dinner with Paul twice a week. She had even begun to cook for her woman's husband occasionally. They had plenty of take-outs as well—pasta and fried chocolate cheese cake were their favorite.

At the end of every dinner, she would direct Paul to jerk off and rub his cum over her breasts. She believed his cum was a great skin-protein. She intends to recommend it to her doctor one day. No more sexual intercourse. No more DIP (dick in pussy) either. She was now in control of her destiny and her pussy. She had become the master of bait and switch with Paul. She was now the mistress in-charge of the joyful and probably the agony of Paul's life.

Paul wasn't aware that his ship was sinking, and Sheila was watching him slowly going down from the banks of the river. Paul's greediness and lust were rapidly catching up with him. He was so blind to a forbidden love, so much so that he couldn't see the freight train approaching him at full speed.

Paul wanted more of Sheila. She knew it and was ready to accommodate him for the greater good she saw on the horizon: to be with Pat in the end.

One Thursday evening as Paul was preparing to catch a late flight to Texas, he told Sheila after their early dinner date that he wanted more than just licking her nipples and what else she was offering.

"Sheila, I want more, otherwise, I would prefer to end the affair," he said forcefully like a man in-charge of his destiny.

Paul was desperate and had just dared Sheila. By his action, he had made the biggest mistake of his life to-date with a woman he refused to understand and accept for what she is.

In a cool, sultry, and calculated manner, Sheila unbuttoned her tight blouse to expose her cleavage and raised one of her legs on the arm of the dining room chair for the full view of Paul to see her great assets and said, "Paul, I'm equally tired of your endless promises. I'm tired of the goalless games you're playing. Honestly, I'm sick of your free access to both of us."

Sheila knew Paul was desperate, greedy, and bluffing. She knew his mind is mushy, soft, and irrational, to say the least. To her, Paul must be out of his fucking mind because this puppy of a man, this pussy-whipped of a man, must have forgotten that she had the sex tapes, and much more.

She was in control. Paul just refused to get it through his thick head, so far . . . but again, he had been thinking only with his body parts between his legs, since the beginning.

"Paul, I have a copy of the tapes, in case you have forgotten. I'm sure you still have yours too."

Then, Sheila playing the role of Mrs. Paradine in the movie *The Paradine Case*, looked into Paul's eyes and took advantage of his lust for her the same way Mrs. Paradine took advantage of her spellbound defense lawyer, Gregory Peck.

This time, however, Sheila acted even better like a seasoned Hollywood star—she moved closer to Paul with her cleavage almost touching his chin, the same way Ophelia (Jamie Lee Curtis) did, showing her cleavage to Clarence Beeks (Gleason), during the train ride, in the movie, *Trading Places*.

Sheila composed herself and softly presented Paul her counteroffer and said, Pat, I mean, Paul, these are my list of demands if you want to taste my kitty Kat again. I mean, my pussy, in case you don't know what that means.

> *Change the lock of your main door and give me a copy. I don't want any uninvited guest when I'm there, except your lovely housemaid.*
>
> *I want us to be together, every other weekend, starting from this weekend.*
>
> *I want breakfast in bed, when I spend the weekend and give me pleasure on demand as your mistress.*
>
> *My car is ten years old and I want one of those new 2012 Ford electric hybrid Bolts.*
>
> *I want my hair and nails done once a week.*

I want my own debit card linked to your account with agreed upon budget per month. Let's start with a thousand dollar a month for the next six months.

I want my gym life time membership paid in full, like your fucking wife.

I want flowers sent to my office once a week and simply signed PP. FYI, I love lilies.

I know you have disobeyed me and continue to fuck your wife. Henceforth, I want that to stop. For all I know, she is probably fucking the entire police department. Your dick, tongue, and lips are mine now for good. I want you to stay closer to home in case I need you on demand to lick me when I'm wet . . . I do make pussy house calls . . . I will make those calls on your ass . . .

You need to check-in with me before you schedule any of your fucking trips to Texas. No more impromptu visit to Texas. After all, you have no child with the bitch . . .

I'm now your official mistress or as you called me the other day, "My nasty whore." You will take care of me . . . unless you want the tapes to go viral.

Paul, it's your call not mine. You made your bed, now you will lay on it. I'm ready to let you go down whenever you are ready, dead or alive . . .

She sips a little wine and then took off her tank top to show Paul her "In your face cleavage." She uncrossed her legs slowly, and sexually winked at Paul and said, "Paul, this is not blackmail by any means. I'm only utilizing the facts and evidence of the events in which you were an active participant. I'm giving you a taste of your destiny you had formulated and desired. You wanted me. Ok, I'll let you have all of me for now, provided you behave yourself and obey me. One last thing, the terms of this agreement may change at my own discretion and without notice."

All Paul said was, "OK, diamond mistress."

She handed over her cell phone to Paul and said, "Call the bitch on her private cell phone and cancel your flight tonight, and maybe I'll consider your request to fuck me—leave the phone on speaker, I want to hear her voice. By the way, here is an agreement for your signature as you speak to her . . . Sign it, my dear. I'm sick of you men screwing me over."

Paul did as he was told. Sheila's pussy and the rest of her body parts had made Paul's brain clouded and mushy.

The only question Pat had for her husband for his sudden change of their weekend arrangements was, "Whose cell number was that?" Paul lied like a pro, and said, "It's my new cell number. Sheila has been calling me nonstop wanting to get in touch with you."

Sheila smiled, kissed Paul on the forehead, and whispered in his ear, "Good boy, you did well for your sake. Now you can use your dick to play on the outer wall of my pussy while you talk to that thing."

She then shifted position and lifted her other leg over the love seat and said, "Puky, be on your knees, follow my directives and work me over. Enjoy your reward because you had earned it for today, greedy boy." She was saving Pat's cell number, under "SistaP" at the same time Paul was pleasuring her.

Sheila was great. She wished her high school drama teacher could see her now in full operation. Mr. Spike Lee, where art thou?

Sheila then said aside, "What Pat thought she left behind will soon follow her just as the shell follows the snail. Thank you Jesus."

Paul's dick was erect, hard, and at full strength ready to enter Sheila's pussy when suddenly and abruptly Sheila stood and bid Paul goodnight. "Puky, don't bother to get up, I know my way out," she said, as she walked away galloping into the night. She made sure Paul was deprived of his girls that evening. She was mean and unforgiving. She loved her acts . . .

Paul couldn't justify what had become of him. "What alternative do I have," was what he was asking his dysfunctional mind. He was determined but helpless, at best. He refused to see his contribution to his own misery and the deep hole he was digging for himself and everyone around him.

"Let those without fault, cast the first stone," he repeated aloud again and again to convince himself that he may be jumping into a bottomless pit, he is willing to accept the consequences of his actions.

His peaceful life was rapidly crashing like a glacial melting rapidly due to global warming.

The family he nurtured for nearly sixteen years was now falling apart and no one was able or capable of stopping it. He has just lost control of his own faculty. He accepted that much now.

———————————————— •◉• ————————————————

Pat was spending more time to adjust to her new position in Warsaw, Texas. She was spending less and less time in addressing the voids in her marriage. She mostly thought of her marital problems only when she was tired after work and wanted to be beside her husband for relaxation, love, warmth, sex, company for social events, and a little comfort, on lonely nights. She wasn't ready to explore another man, as backup, so soon.

Finding a date or a de-facto sex mate as a chief of police was not easy even when the thought came to her mind numerous times. She blamed that to being a public figure. Considering her past, she must also be careful, calculated, and thread gently.

CHAPTER 13

After speaking with her husband on one of her weekends off, Pat bid him good night. The same late Friday, she changed her mind and decided at 4:55 pm, to make a surprise visit to her husband at OldPort, and took the last flight. Innocently, she was being considerate. After all, her husband had sacrificed a lot for her and she thought her husband might be getting tired of making the new fortnight trip arrangement to Warsaw, Texas. She had no knowledge of the agreement Paul had signed, under duress, with Sheila for the newly imposed visiting rights, privileges, and change of schedules.

Instead of calling Paul to pick her up at the airport, she rented a car at the airport and drove to her once peaceful and happy domicile on the beautiful Bay. In a way, she was happy to be back for the short visit.

At the back of her mind, she suspected her husband might be up to something or possibly having an affair since he had a new cell number without any other legitimate reasons other than "Sheila had been calling." What's more, Pat had dialed the same number many times and no one answered it. Although she could trace the cell number to find out the true owner, she decided that it wasn't worth her time.

Sheila, on the one hand, only answered Paul's coded cell number stored with his picture on her new private number registered under Paul's account, her unofficial girlfriend's husband. She suspected Pat might call the line; therefore, she only answered Paul's calls. Dealing with Pat directly at the right time was her only option—she was following her plan B to the letters.

On the other hand, Sheila was the last person on Pat's mind. After all, "She prefers women," she concluded, considering how she had pursued her before and after their last encounter.

As she turned off the highway towards her house, she had a flash back to February 5th. She immediately erased that day from her mind.

At this juncture, she had no intention of confronting her husband's infidelity. Even, if her intuition turned out to be true, she had no more energy to pursue any self-inflicted wounds any longer. The legal encounters she had with Sheila and her husband, Ted Samson, had drained her valuable energy. If she found what she suspected to be true, she wasn't ready to deal with such nightmare. At last, she has embarked on a new philosophy for life: work with what life offers, improve on it, if possible, move on, and leave the rest to the Lord.

She breathed a sigh of relief when she saw there was no other car parked in front of their home. All the lights were off except the ones in the den and the kitchen.

She parked her rental car and walked gently towards the front door without carrying her luggage or purse. She was really anxious and happy to be home and be with her husband. However, before she attempted to open the door, she could hear laughter inside the house and the aroma of curry-chicken, circulating the air outside the door.

Nervously, she inserted her key into the front door and turned it. Alas, her key couldn't unlock her own home. "What the hell," she said aloud.

The lock had been changed two weeks earlier under the directive of Sheila. Sheila was now in the driver's seat since Pat left. For all practical purposes, Mr. and Mrs. Peterman were no longer in-charge of their own destiny, by their own design.

Pat started pounding at the door saying, "Paul, open the darn door. I know you're in there."

She instantly recollected how Ted might have felt on the night of February 5th. Déjà Vu.

Unrehearsed, after two minutes of intentional delay, Sheila walked to the door with a glass of white wine. She was wearing only an eye-popping bra, a silk camisole to embellish her chest, and stilettos. She opened the door and said, "Oh, it's you Pat, come on in, dear."

This time around, Pat followed Sheila to the den of her own home where Paul's hands were tied to the chair behind his back, half naked, blind-folded, and caramel rubbed over his nipples and . . .

"What the hell was going on in my house . . . ?" was all Pat could ask.

Pat composed herself and recounted the way she had responded to Sheila's husband, Ted Samson, on February 5, when she wasn't at the receiving end. She recited "Serenity now" in her mind. She would need it and much more.

Her latest readings on African proverbs taught her also that, "A moment of patience can prevent a great disaster and a moment of impatience can ruin a whole life." Pat knew her old ways would be less traveled this time. She must now proceed rationally in an irrational circumstance. She now wished she had been privileged with this wisdom on the night of her fifteenth year wedding anniversary.

Pat couldn't utter a word. She was speechless and stunned by Sheila's audacity to take over her house and the man she still considers her husband. She has now become a guest in her own house.

"What goes around comes around," Sheila was murmuring.

Ted would've loved to witness what would transpire next—act four, scene two.

Sheila quickly finished her drink and handed over the glass to Pat. She kissed Paul on the lips, and without recognizing Pat's presence, said:

Welcome to our home, attorney Peterman. What a surprise. It seems you have violated your own restraining order. Let me say thanks for dropping the charges against my husband. FYI, Ted is in the psycho ward or in the experts' parlance; he has been in therapy at the military hospital's mental ward since you dropped the charges. By the way, here are my own sets of keys to your house since I don't intend to disturb your stay with my Puky this weekend or for how long you may be staying. You've decided to use my time with our man. You owe me one. And you will pay. Count on it.

Lest I forget Madam, your restraining order is no longer valid. I had checked. Last time, when I delivered the flowers, I wasn't invited. This time around, I'm a special guest of Mr.

Paul Peterman, whose name is also on the mortgage. As a lawyer, you already know his rights. Now, deal with that, Ms. Attorney, your Highness, Madam Commissioner, or whatever you call yourself nowadays.

She wanted to provoke Pat. She wanted to get under her skin. Thank heavens, Pat didn't take the bait. What's more, Sheila refused to untie Paul or removed his blind fold. The caramel was melting and running down Paul's private section. It was actually appetizing and ready to be . . .

Sheila was cool and calculated as she recounted the famous proverb that said, "Why take away something by force which you can obtain by love?"

"Sooner or later, Pat will be mine. She just doesn't know it yet," she said aside.

Pat could never think of what just transpired live, in front of her, in a million years.

Sheila then asked Pat to open the car garage so that she could recover her brand new Ford electric Bolt. She wanted her to see her new ride. The license plate read, "Sheila-PP." One P is a credit to Paul. The other P is a credit to Pat, or vice-versa. It seemed, Sheila was stuck on PPs. After all, Paul had told her that her new car had been purchased from a joint account with his wife. She just wanted to give credit to her private philanthropists . . .

Actually, Paul had withdrawn the money from his 401(k) retirement account to pay cash for the purchase, to hide the paper trail from his wife. After all, he will deal with the tax consequences when they file their 2012 tax returns. However, the probability of filing a joint return is less than one percent, considering their current state of affairs.

Pat refused to obey Sheila's command to open the garage door. Instead, she untied Paul and removed his blind fold and let him do his own dirty work. She refused Sheila's control over her. She never saw Sheila's fine car partially paid for by her hard earned money.

Sheila walked to her car, turned the ignition key, backed up to the driveway, stopped, and let it idle for about five minutes. Behind the wheel, she contemplated her next move. With her hand on the ignition key, she wasn't certain if her plan is working, considering the conflicts developing among the three remaining gang of four: Pat, Paul, and Sheila. She felt lonely. The only result, certain, for her actions, to-date, was her estranged mental husband and detached children. What's more, Mr. and attorney Peterman were still together possibly attempting to reconcile their damaged marriage behind closed door, probably to mess with her mind—she knew divorces between the rich and important people don't happen easily. As she sat behind the wheel, she was questioning her own resolve. She really never considered Pat visiting her home without Paul's knowledge.

Minutes later, she stepped out of her car with the engine still running and walked back to the front door of the Petermans. She wanted to apologize and say her goodbyes. To her, enough was enough. She knocked at the door a couple of times but the commotions between Mr. and Mrs. Peterman, going on inside their home, convinced her to get the hell out and fast. She didn't want to risk being arrested like her husband, even when she knew Pat would not take that route again. What's more, Pat had lost the protection and preferential treatments of her colleagues at the local police department.

She got back into her car as quickly as possible. Before driving off, she took a CD from her collections, a live version of Isaac Hayes' *I stand accused,* and placed it on the windshield of Pat's leased car with a note, "For Patty, from Sheila. Oh, call your lawyer, if you dare to as you did when you received my flowers. I'm not done with you yet, my love."

She wasn't ready to accept defeat. She wanted to try her last strategy: Plan C. If that failed, she would end her pursuits and accept that her God had forsaken her.

As she was driving away, she started to miss Pat as never before. She thought of going back to the home of Mr. Peterman and rescued her love from the tyranny of Paul because any action against Pat was against her. The pains of Pat had become her pains. She almost felt responsible for the current rancor taking place now at the Petermans.

"Patience Sheila, your plan is working," she told herself. The unplanned Pat's visit has just become a blessing in disguise.

She smiled and said, "I'll have that bitch soon. Paul is fucked, and on his way out." She had successfully used similar exit strategy to get rid of her own husband, Ted—she had planned for Ted to see her with Pat the day Ted lost his fucking mind. She had finished him off with her one-sided speech. Now, fate had made Pat's impromptu visit to her own home saw her with her husband, Paul. She suspected such visit might happen later, which was all the more reason she demanded the change of the house keys. She just never thought it will be this soon. This time, Paul will be next to go. Better yet, she would safe Pat from her husband on a rebound. Genius!

———————————— •●• ————————————

That same evening, Pat took a cab back to the airport and caught the last flight back to Warsaw. She had had enough.

She finally accepted her marriage to be over. She had not forgotten her rental car still parked in front of her home, she was just not in any emotional shape to drive back to the airport under the circumstances. She never saw Sheila's CD or the note.

Paul saw the CD the following morning. He was the right beneficiary, after all.

Pat couldn't shed tears anymore. She had known the end was near. She just never thought the end would be this soon. She never thought her love for her husband would evaporate so quickly. She had finally come face to face with her own demon. To her, all the relationship experts, all the sex experts, all the collective books on "How to Make Your Marriage Work in the 21st century," were all for naught.

Unconsciously, however, by leaving her own home due in part to Sheila's presence, that evening, is like "Punishing a fish by throwing it into the water." Finally, everyone and everything were playing nicely into Sheila's hand.

Paul drank himself to sleep that evening. At dusk, the following day, he drove directly to Sheila's house and practically forced himself on her.

On his way out, he told Sheila, "I hope you have a tape of what had just transpired because as I had said repeatedly, you're my mistress and my whore. Henceforth, I'll fuck you when I want, and how I want it. From now on, I'm in-charge of that fucking pussy and your ass."

As he walked away, Sheila smiled, hissed, and said aloud, "In your dreams, buster." She was always cool and calculated like that. So far, she was winning the lover's war between the three parties. There wasn't any need for her to overreact to

Paul's childish rant. "The fool will fall by the wayside sooner than I thought," she concluded. She went and took a long hot bath . . . For all practical purposes, she had a great evening.

Sheila couldn't believe how perfectly Paul's actions were fitting into her new plan.

She even loved the sex for the first time with Paul. The sex encounter was intense. It was rough. Sheila smiled and said to herself, "That mother-fucker is damn good when he is pissed and determined. Maybe, he would get his mojo back with the right woman."

Paul was obviously losing control of his senses. He had forgotten he is still a married man claiming lame authority over his wife's potential want-to-be lover. But again, given the fact that his marriage might be over, under the circumstances, nothing mattered to him any longer.

"At 42, Paul was still Mama's boy and losing his mind for a pussy he can only sample, and may never be his," Sheila said to herself. Again, she always knew her pussy was an aphrodisiac to anyone that tasted or had it. Paul was the recent recipient. Ted was the last beneficiary or victim, whichever the case may be.

In a way, she didn't want Paul's dick, the same way she wasn't jubilant about the dick of her soon to be ex-husband, Ted Samson. She had tolerated Ted's dick just to bear him two children. She could count the number of sexual intercourse with him during their seventeen years of marriage. Her number was less than fifty-nine including anniversaries and special events: mother's day, birthday (his), wedding day anniversary, father's day, and recently, the Obama victory's day. Page 115 of her diary, under "Sex encounters with Ted," documented it all . . .

Paul's dick wasn't the type she wanted either. She would have preferred a strap-on, if she had to choose. With a strap-on, she could choose the length and circumference of the penis. Paul's penis wasn't of that specimen. His dick wasn't long enough, not long lasting enough, and definitely non-adjustable to fit any size she wanted.

Sheila recalibrated and reviewed her strategy of how to accelerate her connection with Pat one last time. One great thing about her was this—she makes her plans flexible. She wanted to optimize her pursuit of Pat when the blood is still fresh in the water. To her, Paul was just acting out. "He didn't have what it takes to control me more than what I would allow. He was so mediocre, at best," she lamented. She knows she was Paul's cupcake with cream on top, and he was the greedy boy who would do anything to eat it. "What a greedy little lamb," she reiterated.

Paul never told Sheila that Pat had gone back to Texas the previous night.

The following Thursday, Sheila left a message on Paul's cell, telling him she wouldn't be entertaining him for her next weekend with him since he was incapable of controlling his wife or properly managed his sexual affairs. "Paul, you made a bad choice by your ineptitude and indecisions. Above all, you are inconsiderate, selfish, and greedy. As your punishment, you will not have me for a while, if at all. More importantly, I'm suspending my pussy encounters with your tail since you continue to fuck your wife. I'm certain you did her the other night when she came and used my allotted time against my instruction and directives. I hope you enjoyed how you had it with me last week because it may be your last chance to poke this pussy."

And to emphasize her resolve, she told him emphatically, "One more thing, I don't consider myself welcomed in your house any more since I no longer have my own sets of keys anyway." To nail his coffin, she sent him a clear and crisp picture of her cleavage and a long black dildo, the size of a delicious frozen Italian sausage, between her breasts, with the caption, "Take your last peak for your memory Puky, and bye for good." What a smooth operator . . .

Paul immediately called her back to let her know he's on his way to drop her duplicate keys to his family Mansion. He could only leave a message as well. At this point, they were both ignoring each other's calls. Her strategy worked. And again, it wasn't a surprise—she was that good . . .

Forty minutes and ten seconds later, Paul was at Sheila's door with her set of keys, inside a sealed love-greeting card and a dozen lilies. He pressed her intercom and announced his presence. Treating Paul like a total stranger with a nonchalant demeanor, she answered, "Paul, you are not invited, what the heck do you want?"

"Babe, I want to return your keys."

"I'm about to take my bath. You can wait, or just put the keys under the doormat. Better yet, mail me the damn thing," she fired back. She then went on and said, "I had told you never to call me, Babe, the same thing you call your fucking wife." Sheila was on a roll and enjoying every minute of her cute self. All women worth their salt should take a page from her playing book. Caution: only if you are willing to go to hell with her when all is said and done . . .

Paul had wanted to elaborate the other reasons he was reporting for an unscheduled duty. He pleaded with her to let him in, and offered to give her the bath. All she did was switched off the intercom and ignored his ass.

When Sheila finished her warm bath, twenty-eight minutes later, she looked outside her window and saw Paul standing beside his car; with a bouquet of flowers clutched to his chest, and looking directly at her door, as if an FBI agent was on a stake out for one of America's most wanted. With a pink towel wrapped around her chest, Sheila opened the door, immediately turned around, and walked away without acknowledging his presence. Paul followed, as she walked upstairs, while watching her butt bouncing in rhythms— in a dramatic boogety boogie style. Sheila knew he was watching . . . she just loved how she let her butt does her talking . . . She knows how to position herself for a maximum impact. Many, who might consider her acts narcissistic, would also unanimously agree that she knew how to work her assets effectively. She should have majored in marketing or advertising, instead of accounting—what a waste of priceless assets, what a misallocation of nature's resources.

Her theatrics were working. Smiling and still not acknowledging Paul's presence, she said, "Leave the keys on the kitchen table and leave. Have a great day, Mr. Peterman."

Paul ignored her instruction and followed her to her balcony. He grabbed her on her shoulders, turned her around, and started to kiss her forcefully. At first, she resisted but succumbed seconds later and kissed him back. As her waist towel fell to the ground, he continued to palm her breasts, squeezed her butt, and attempted to finger fuck her. Her pussy was already wet, very wet, and ready. His hand was drenched with her nectar.

"Not here, Puky Please. Not here, the neighbors might be watching," Sheila cautioned with her signature brown and big sexy eyes. Her breathing was becoming heavier and accelerating each passing second. She closed her eyes and tried to regain her composure but couldn't. She was getting weak by the second.

Truly, Paul got the message from their previous encounter that Sheila loved it rough. Too bad Ted never took the time to take charge of his wife, bi-sexual or not.

Paul carried her to her bed, laid her on her back, and started to kiss every part of her body. As he attempted to get up and pull down his jeans, Sheila, now hot, wet, wanting, and gasping for air, as if, she was ready to have a ten pound baby, pulled him back and said," Lick me. I'm wet and juicy, as you like it."

Instead, Paul disobeyed and ignored her once again. Unzipping his pant only, he pinned her down by her shoulders, and used his legs to spread her legs as far apart as they can go. She attempted to push him away but unsuccessful. His gym membership is paying off nicely.

Paul's action reminded her of the scene in the movie *Goldfinger* and the flirting encounter between Sean Connery and Honor Blackman (Pussy Galore) in the barn of Auric Goldfinger.

The only difference was that Paul did even better with Sheila—he fucked her hard. Very hard, like a wounded tiger fighting for his dear life from Kenyan poachers.

When he was satisfied and done with the missionary position, he turned her around and fucked her doggy-style. It was the second for him. His first was with her during his wedding day anniversary. She loved it. She responded passionately, as if possessed by the Holy Ghost. For the first time, she called out his name, "Paul, please don't hurt me. My gash, you are poking my uterus. I'm sorry Paul. Shit, I want you too . . ."

Twenty minutes later, both reached orgasm. They collapsed and were speechless under the ceiling fan circulating only warm air. She softly asked Paul to get her a drink of water and a warm wet face towel. She wanted more of Paul; once she could catch her breathe. Instead, Paul stood up, zipped up his pant, left his house keys on her dresser, and walked away with only one sentence, "I hope you have all that on digital." Oh yah, the rubber finally met the road perfectly this time around. Paul had just represented all men at the Olympics and won a gold medal . . .

All Sheila could say about Paul not acknowledging her passion and sexual cooperation was, "Mother-fucker."

Frankly, Paul earned that title: Sheila was a mother of two and he had just fucked her.

As Paul was driving home, he said to himself, "Two can play that game, bitch." He was truly in love with her . . .

Temporarily, it seemed the real Paul was back, alive, and well. Finally, he had found what his heart desired. In Sheila, he found the challenges, the dreams, the passion, the fun, the fantasies, and the true satisfaction he had missed with his own estranged wife. "She would be mine in due time," he concluded.

CHAPTER 14

The following Friday morning, Sheila took a taxi to the airport for the first flight to Houston International Airport. Upon her arrival, she lodged at the famous Warsaw International Airport Hotel and dialed Pat's number already stored in her cell phone.

"Hi Paul, can I help you?" Pat answered. She recognized the number from Paul's last call at Sheila's command.

"Pat, this is Sheila; I'm here at the airport hotel in the bridal suite. I would like to go over mutual concerns with you this evening. See you then." Before Pat could respond and ask how Sheila got her number, she hung up. Passive aggressiveness was also her specialty.

Sheila changed into what she knew Pat would like to see on her and waited for the love of her life to arrive. At this juncture, she wasn't afraid of any consequences. She was convinced, if history was any guide; Pat was helpless to do anything irrational or stupid.

If she went down, Pat would be on the same ride with her. Among the parties involved, she had the least to lose. She was ready to lose whatever she had. She reiterated one more time the African proverb, "Use people who have something to gain, not people with nothing to lose."

After all, Sheila had left the husband she never loved and disconnected with her children she never wanted. Her career was unimportant and Pat was all that would make her whole. She had become addicted to Pat and was determined to have her exclusively, with all she has to offer.

That evening, Pat was a "No show." Sheila was jealously upset but calm, calculated, and in control. She couldn't sleep all night. She called Pat's number several times, there was no answer. She thought as much. She was not an idiot.

The next morning, she ordered a dozen white roses and a box of Pat's favorite imported chocolate bars. She included a note in her own hand writing and a video tape of their brunch together the first time they met at the café on the Boulevard . . .

Her note read in part, "Pat, you stood me up last night. I'll forgive you this time because you're just confused right now from the shock and all the love around you. Maybe, you were still pissed off at me because of what transpired in your house in OldPort last week. Let's work together this time. The choice is yours, my dear. I've come here for you in peace and for you alone. I can't wait to give you more . . ."

She included another hand written card she had kept over the years from her former college roommate/lover, B. Johnson. M, and added her own comments to be melodramatic, "Pat, here is what you're missing. I'm here for you:"

> Sitting on your desk . . .
> legs wide open . . .
> 45 degree angle . . .
> oozing . . .
> frothing . . .
> foaming . . .

moaning . . .
wailing . . .
summoning you . . .
begging you . . .
No! No! No!
Commanding you to
Lick me, lick me now!!!
Flick your tongue . . .
quench your thirst . . . douse the flames . . .
extinguish the fire that rages between my thighs!!!
Come and get it. It was made especially for you . . .
I'll repay my ecstasy and satisfaction in kind as
well. Let's call it reciprocity . . .

Sheila just wanted to set the right mood for the second
meeting that she knew must be sooner than later.

She didn't plan to be in Warsaw more than two days. Her
office business partners were now demanding explanations
for her low productivity and office appointment cancelations.
Her career was sliding into the abyss. She needed to return
home and make the final plan for her uncertain future.

On her way to the airport, she drafted another letter to Pat
that simply said:

*I'm doing my best right now to work with you.
I have tolerated the way you're treating me for
your lack of love and understanding. I don't
understand how such an intelligent lady can be
so naïve and simple minded.*

*This time, I won't overreact as you did in the
past. We'll be together. I have reserved myself
for you.*

FYI: Paul is out. Pat, you're in. Or do you prefer both of us? Paul has tried so hard to have me, but all I have voluntarily allowed him to do was lick me.

The morning after you came to town, he came to my house and practically raped me. That was the first time he fucked me without you present. Now, I truly believe you, and know how you felt, when you accused Ted of the date rape.

Girlfriend, the men in our lives are no good for us. It's time we bond together and stand by each other . . . no matter what.

I'll be back next week. You need time to think things over . . . ; we need each other more than ever, my love. With God's blessing, we'll be family soon. I'm in love with you.

I've one life. I'm ready to give it to you. My life is yours whenever you want it. So far, your actions towards me are only a bump on the road. I'll be back, love. I'll be back. I promise.

The package was sent to Pat's office by private courier service with return receipt required.

CHAPTER 15

Upon her return to OldPort airport, Sheila called Paul to pick her up so that she could spend the night with him. He was furious. He wanted to know where the heck she had been for the last three days. He controlled his emotions because of the uncontrollable love he had for her. He had put his phone on automatic redial for the last twenty four hours but could only leave messages. Half the night, her phone had busy signal. He hardly had any sleep. For the last three days, he had driven to her house many times and knocked at her door because her car was parked outside. He went to her office, as early as six in the morning, and waited at the parking lot to see if she would show up at the office . . . no luck. On the third day, he drove to her house again—now his daily ritual. Fortunately for him, a thin Korean looking curly hair teenager, mowing a neighbor's lawn, advised him, "Sir, I think she is not in. I saw her in a taxi two days ago, and as you can see, her car had been parked at the same spot." The poor boy had admired Sheila many times like the rest of his friends with raging hormones. He had seen Paul during his previous daily drive runs. He also recognized Paul from previous encounter when he saw him purchasing a park of condom and a pack of gum at his father's convenience store, a few weeks earlier. During school days, he works four hours after school, and twelve hours a day, during weekends and holidays.

"Did you misplace your damn phone?" Paul asked Sheila, as he was placing her luggage in the back seat.

Sheila ignored him and his question. To her, Paul was only a doormat and a means to an end. He was only useful for one purpose or maybe two, at the most. According to her, all Paul had that was valuable was his tongue to oblige her on demand, until . . .

Any dick encounters with Paul were only a stop-gap and temporary pleasures she was forced to enjoy for the greater good—Pat.

As soon as they got on the highway, she removed her jacket and started rubbing Paul's bulging rod between his legs. She sure knew how to tease him senselessly. If he was mad at her for the past few days, he wasn't showing it any longer. The power of Sheila over him is beyond his control. He really can't help himself. No one had been able to . . .

She softly said in her usual manner, "Paul, this is my agenda from this point forward: never ask me where I've been. I'll tell you when and how I need you. Your primary duty is to make yourself available on demand. It seems I'm fucking repeating myself like a broken record; your obligation is to be on call and ever ready when I want you. Can you do that or that's too much for you to handle, Puky?"

Paul only smiled and kept driving at full speed without a word. Getting home in earnest is his problem of the moment. He had missed her for the past three days.

She unbuttoned the first few top buttons of her blouse and continued to show her vintage assets. She then said, "My pussy has been moist for three days and uncared for. I'm sure you want to taste it. It's all yours tonight, if you could only learn to shut the hell up and stop asking silly questions. By the way, you're becoming a pro licking me. I think I taught you well. If you must know, you definitely earned a C+, thus far."

Paul interrupted her with a fake smile while looking at her cleavage and said, "Only a C+ after all . . ."

"Just pay attention to the road and drive," Sheila fired back.

She was doing all she could to piss off Paul, hoping he would leave her alone. Unfortunately, the more she tried such strategy, the more Paul became attracted to her, and the more he wanted her. She never wanted any emotional connection to him. She didn't want him to end up like her soon-to-be ex, Ted, who for all practical purpose had lost his mind. When all is said and done, she has a soul, no matter how shallow.

So far, Paul wasn't taking the bait. He was becoming a pro handling her as well. Quid quo pro . . .

To him, a woman with her quality, a woman with her beauty, a woman who could give him what he wanted, deserves to be in command and in control. This was one of the few times opposites attract, absolutely. Sheila was actually playing into his hands. At least, that was what was going through his demented and hollow head.

For any rational onlooker, Paul's brain had been clouded with impossible dreams. His thoughts were no longer his own. He could no longer control his actions. With the exemption of one of his body parts, the rest of him was becoming soft. Thank goodness, his functioning body part was still perfect and ever ready, whenever he thought of her. Thanks to Sheila, his most prized possession was even getting better, stronger, more turgid, and long lasting with each encounter with her. He didn't need any erectile dysfunction drugs. Thanks heavens.

Sheila had had a fruitless trip to Texas. To let Paul lick her for the rest of the night might compensate her a little, at least, for the unproductive visit. At the same time, she wanted to reduce her stress from dealing with Pat's disappointment. "What a price I have to pay before Pat comes to her senses and be with me," she told herself.

Frankly, she was mostly nauseous whenever she slept with Paul. He would never be her desired specimen. No man ever did.

The raw dick of a man never excited her. Her preference for Pat was personal, out of necessity, and nothing against Paul, the puppy of a man.

She turned around, placed her left leg behind his back, and wrapped it around his waist. She then placed her right leg underneath his legs, as Paul drove at top speed to get home in earnest.

"Slow down and concentrate, unless you want to kill both of us and kiss this wet pussy good bye, greedy boy," she calmly told him.

With her leopard bra showing her eye popping cleavage in full view, she said, "One more reminder Puky dear, stay away from your house-cleaning slot, Angie, or what the heck her name is. What's her fucking fake name on her work permit again? Or did she have a work permit? Well, it doesn't matter. She doesn't seem to like me much. Frankly, I don't give a fuck about her either. Hope you had been using condoms. You ought to know her people can procreate by just kissing . . . You have your hands full already . . ."

Sheila was just fishing for reasons to be mean to Paul. The relationship between Paul and Angelika was circumstantial to anyone familiar with Paul's household. If truth be told, the only time Paul and Angie did it, with condom, was after a massage she gave Paul when he was tipsy after Sheila refused to see him many months ago. Angie wanted to continue the puppy affair but Paul would only agree to have sex with her only if he could use condom. Angelika refused. She wanted to give Paul a son they once discussed during their emotional get-to-know each other talks, during their first sex encounter. If Angie was cross examined under oath, her version of their association would be entirely different from Paul's.

Sheila had a joyful night if allowing Paul to do what she wanted was considered as such. The tongue of Pat would have been her choice of preference that evening.

Paul had settled for whatever Sheila offered. However, he knew how to pick his battle. To a detached observer, Paul had sold his soul to the devil when Satan was celebrating birthday with the faithful. So far, Paul was operating on his only game plan: plan X.

CHAPTER 16

The following Wednesday, Sheila flew back to Texas to meet Pat for the last time. She was determined. She cared less whether Pat was fired from her new job or not. She wouldn't allow Pat to ignore her twice in a row. To her, Pat must have lost her senses and moral compass to think she can ignore her forever. She was determined to achieve her goal this time around. She was at the driver's seat. She even felt it in her marrow. The only life she wanted to live was the life where Pat sojourned. Her plan C was engaged and active. It was her final plan.

Before leaving OldPort, she didn't know if she would be back or not. She took a month long absence from her job for family reasons. Her excuse was that her twenty-year old daughter had eloped with a foreign business tycoon, three times her age, and she needed to find her and rescue her. She was such a liar. Her daughter was only nineteen, a virgin, well and alive, at her present overpopulated public university, a marketable difference from her former cozy Ivy League.

Nothing meant much to her any longer. Material things meant little to her. She was obsessed and addicted to Pat. She was in love, and she would pay any price to have, and hold that love, period. This time, she was well armed, determined, and desperate. Usually, patience with love was her weapon of choice. With plan C, she had abandoned that philosophy as unproductive.

Upon her arrival at the Warsaw International airport, she called Pat and wanted to inform her where she will be staying for the week or until further notice. Of course, as expected, she wasn't able to leave any messages. She then called the information desk at the police headquarters to ascertain if Pat is still in her office and for how long—they told her more information she wanted . . . there goes privacy and security details of a public official.

That late afternoon, she packed the gift Pat couldn't refuse. Contained therein was the part one, on DVD with audio illustration, their threesome encounters, on February 5th.

Sheila was the narrator on the tape. Even without the video, her voice was sexy and mesmerizing. Also, included in her gift package were a dozen panties she wanted Pat to wear whenever they get together and five strapless bras similar but better than the one Pat wore on the night of their February encounter, courtesy of the stranger from Victoria's secret.

A note was attached, instructing Pat to keep the DVD as her copy.

The note also stated that she had kept her own copy of the DVD with her lawyer, in case it would be necessary for future litigation or any other reasons. She didn't regard her actions as a threat, she was simply determined, and must have whatever she wanted on this trip. She had had enough of Pat's childish and nonsense behavior. In her life to-date, this was the only time she has to work this hard for what she wanted. But again, Pat was special to her. She is worth waiting for. She is worth the efforts and sacrifices . . .

With the package, she included a note, "This is only part one of the movie. Please, enjoy it at your leisure. I hope you enjoy it as much as I do each time I watch it whenever I miss you.

I really hope we can watch it together tonight. I'm yours and you ought to know it."

She ended the note, with a section written within the shape of a heart, "I'll be expecting you for dinner around 6:30pm. Please dear, don't repeat the 'no shows' of last week. I'm fucking tired of chasing you around."

The same special private courier service she had used in the past delivered the package again. It was marked urgent and personal, to Chief Patricia Peterman—to be delivered before 5:00pm. She paid premium for the delivery. Express delivery service to her Boo, at any cost, was worth every cent.

Pat loaded the DVD on her official computer but quickly removed it when she saw the contents. She locked her door as if a secret national security meeting was about to commence. She took a deep breath, closed her eyes, and prayed to her God for guidance.

She picked up her Holy Bible on her credenza and opened the gospel according to Psalm 38:

> *O Lord, rebukes me not in your anger, nor disciplines me in your wrath!*
>
> *For, your arrows have sunk into me, and your hand has come down on me.*
>
> *There is no soundness in my flesh because of your indignation; there is no health in my bone because of my sin.*
>
> *For my iniquities have gone over my head; like a heavy burden, they are too heavy for me.*

My wounds stink and fester because of my foolishness,

I am utterly bowed down and prostrate; all the day I go about mourning.

For my sides are filled with burning, and there is no soundness in my flesh.

I am feeble and crushed; I groan because of the tumult of my heart.

O Lord, all my longing is before you; my sighing is not hidden from you.

My heart throbs; my strength fails me, and the light of my eyes has gone from me.

My friends and companions stand aloof from my plague, and my nearest kin stand far off.

Those who seek my life lay their snares; those who seek my hurt speak of ruin and meditate treachery all day long.

But I am like a deaf man; I do not hear, like a mute man who does not open his mouth.

I have become like a man who does not hear, and in whose mouth are no rebukes.

But for you, O Lord, do I wait; it is you, O Lord my God, who will answer.

For I said, only let them not rejoice over me, who boast against me when my foot slips!

For I am ready to fall, and my pain is ever before me.

I confess my iniquity; I am sorry for my sin.

But my foes are vigorous, they are mighty, and many are those who hate me wrongfully.

Those who render me evil for good accuse me because I follow after good.

Do not forsake me, O Lord! O my God, do not be far from me!

Make haste to help me, O Lord, my salvation!

———————————————— •●• ————————————————

Pat dialed Sheila's number ten minutes later and scheduled a time to meet her at a steakhouse on Main and 69th Street around seven. "I may run a little late," she concluded and hung up without waiting for Sheila to respond. She was equally fed up with Sheila. Her own plan B would now come face to face with Sheila's plan C. "May the best man win. I beg your pardon, may the best woman win," Sheila said to herself.

Sheila smiled after Pat hung up the phone and said aloud, "The bitch is mine. I love her though."

Pat was at the restaurant thirty minutes early with one of her security details in case of "What if" scenarios from Sheila's actions or reactions. "That bitch may not be stable," she concluded.

Within minutes of Pat's arrival, a sexy waitress handed her a note. It read, "Love, I saw you when you came in with your bodyguard. By the way, you look stunning. This is a private matter and I would appreciate it if you would join me in the private room I've reserved for us at the back. You have no reason to worry or be afraid. The only ammunition I have for you is my heart loaded with love."

Pat looked around and saw Sheila standing at the back of the restaurant with her usual beautiful smile. She excused herself from her bodyguard and walked towards her. Sheila wanted to hug her before they sat down, but Pat ignored her gesture and simply said, "Sheila, please have a seat, I have little time to spare."

Sheila took off her jacket to expose her well-choreographed cleavage with a heart shaped gold necklace to match. She also wore a tight designer jean worn specially for the occasion. She always knew how to heat up the oven—Pat's oven, that is. Pat briefly stared at her valuables, gazed at her tight butt for another second, looked straight into her eyes, and said, "Sheila, why the heck are you here and why are you doing this?"

Before Sheila could answer, her cell rang. It was Paul. "Hello Paul. I'm here with Pat. You just have to call me back later dear, or better yet, let me call you when we're finished. Or, would you like to talk to her?"

Paul immediately hung up and cursed Sheila with all the trashy words in the Queen's English dictionary known to Her Majesty's subjects, and many other choice words he had put together for his sweet bitch. For all practical purposes, his life as he knew it before February 5th is coming to an end. He finally found himself to be a third wheel and no longer relevant. He ultimately admitted that he had lost control of his destiny. His hope of any future with Sheila was dashed, just as he had accepted the end with his estranged wife, Pat

By default, Sheila was now in charge of the husband and wife, on her terms, as if she was practicing unofficial polyandry.

A waitress walked up to their table to take their order. "Sweetie, please bring us two glasses of one of your best vintage white Riesling and a plate of fresh strawberries with a dark warm chocolate on the side, and give us a moment to look at the menu," Sheila told the waitress.

As soon as the waitress left, Sheila turned to Pat and asked, "Love, what would you like for dinner?"

On the one hand, Pat was tempted to punch her on the nose for saying "Love" but that would be unbecoming of a police chief. She had learned her lesson. On the other hand, Sheila was gorgeous, sexy, and under the right circumstances, she would have loved to have her for dinner right there on the dining room table.

Pat hadn't had sex for almost two months. Eating bonbon, her newly acquired taste, since the night of her anniversary is becoming her desert of choice. She had been thinking of Sheila more and more since her detachment from her husband. It wasn't by any means that she wanted Sheila per se; it was the fact that her soul had been lonely and weak for a while. In her soul, she didn't actually want Sheila; the evil contained therein was just uncompromising under the circumstances.

By honoring this date, she had unconsciously opened ajar the door to the gate of hell against all efforts to avoid the abyss . . . She was at a cross road. Sheila's beauty didn't make matters any better either. All of a sudden, Sheila's presence made her weak and her pussy moist. She started shifting in her seat to release the tension or neutralize the friction between her legs.

Pat looked around the room, looked back at Sheila, and said, "Are you taping all this too?"

Sheila smiled and said, "Of course not, dear. I have enough video collections to make my point. For your information, I've the video of our second meeting at the restaurant. I've the video of your visits to my house, and part two of the video when we were together for your anniversary. For now, I'm done with taping. Maybe at the appropriate time, as you wish, we could make our own memories together."

"Sheila, stop the nonsense and . . ."

The waitress walking towards their table cut off Pat's response and line of thought. Pat picked up her cell and pretended to be checking her e-mails.

As the waitress stood closer to Sheila, Pat looked up and said, "I don't want anything to eat."

Not to be out done, Sheila joined the conversation, and said, "I don't want anything either. Please, bring us one of your best sugar and fat free Southern Smithfield cheesecakes and a side order of strawberries with caramel at room temperature in another bowl. Oh, by the way, this is my sister Pat. I'm visiting from Virginia."

Lately, Sheila had been cravings for cheesecake, caramel, chocolate, water melon, and sex.

The waitress smiled and said, "I can tell, you two look alike, and very beautiful. The carnival is in town and y'all ought to go and see it." The waitress was staring at Sheila's cleavage as if that was the microphone for her voice. In a way, no one in the mist could avoid Sheila's chest. Her full choreographed chest for the occasion was out there for the whole world to see. Drama queen Sheila . . .

That was one of the problems Sheila had with her soon-to-be-ex-husband, Ted, who always wanted her to tone it down a little, especially in public. Her response had always been, "The succulent roses are mine and those who have eyes to see, let them see. Otherwise, they should close their eyes and keep moving. I'm not a pastor's wife."

Sheila ignored the waitress and her unsolicited hospitalities. She also ignored her fruitless flirtation and advances, and said, "Thanks Lena for the info, we will check it out."

In her mind, she was actually saying, "I belong to someone else, bitch." The waitress wasn't all that—she was cute, a little short, maybe twenty pounds overweight, with a take-it-or leave-it chest. Not her type under normal circumstances. Ok, she may consider her and her type for a one night stand, after a bottle of hard liquor, and a month without sex.

All that was going through Sheila's mind was, "All I want to eat right now is Pat's bonbon and the rest of her body. It has been such a long time. But again, the night is still young."

Pat pulled back her chair to avoid her knees touching Sheila's. She almost smiled at the waitress as she wondered if the waitress wanted Sheila. For a brief moment, she wished Sheila would pursue the waitress or vice versa so that she could be left the hell alone. She knew better that Sheila's abrupt change of heart would never happen. She knew Sheila

was addicted to her and her body. She knew Sheila was
through with Paul. She just wished she would leave her the
fuck alone. But she equally wanted her even if for just one
night . . . That had been the cord that linked them together—
her sexual eye opener experience with Sheila, the evening
of February 5. The night she saw the rainbow close and
personal . . .

Sheila adjusted her seat, checked out herself with her
makeup mirror and said, "Pat, to answer your question . . ."
but Pat interrupted her and asked to be excused to go to the
bathroom.

Instead, she walked to the main dining room area and ordered
her bodyguard to go back to the station. "I may call the next
shift for a ride home if I have to. I'm having dinner with my
sister out-of-town," she told the guard.

"Ok Chief. Your sister is gorgeous by the way," the guard told
Pat as he walked over to Sheila and said, "It's my pleasure to
meet you Madam. I hope we meet again, soon."

"I doubt that ever happening," Pat said to herself and returned
to her seat at a compelled and involuntary dinner date with
her sister from Pluto. She had camouflaged her as "My sister
from Virginia" to the rest of the world. What a liar for a card
carrying member of the Fifth Baptist church of Warsaw,
Texas.

Pat sat down, looked directly into Sheila's eyes and continued
her inquiry:

Pat: Sheila, why are you doing this?

Sheila: I miss you

Pat: I bet. That's why you've been screwing my husband's brains out.

Sheila: Paul is nothing to me and you know it. I feel like throwing up each time I've to be with him, but I coped for your sake. By the way, the only time he screwed me was when he practically raped me. Otherwise, I only allowed him to practice his pussy licking on me in the event you ever wanted him to do the same to you the proper way. (Her lying was now becoming her reality)

Pat: I don't give a shit what y'all did or wanted to do to each other.

Sheila: I'm glad you don't care about him because I never wanted him either.

Pat: Sheila, why are you here because I've to go shortly.

Sheila: You look gorgeous and beautiful.

Pat: Never mind that. Why the hell are you bothering me?

Sheila: I love you Pat and I've been miserable without you.

Pat: You came all the way out here to tell me that shit?

Sheila: I wanted to be close to you and make you happy. I want to be happy with you.

Pat: Who told you I'm not happy? FYI, I'm very happy here. I'm getting my life back together and making good and understanding new friends.

Sheila: Are you dating anyone now? I wouldn't blame you if you were.

Pat: That's none of your damn business and you know it.

Sheila: I just want to make you happy.

Pat: Make me happy by blowing up my cell and sending me videos?

Sheila: How do you expect me to get your attention? You have done everything within your power to ignore and get rid of me. You stood me up once and, as I see it, you never wanted to see me until I took this latest drastic step.

Pat: Not by threatening and harassing me at work and trying to destroy my career.

Sheila: Pat, you did that to yourself in OldPort. You cannot blame me for that. I wasn't the one who called the cops. I wasn't the one who refused to drop the charges. I'm just not about to pay you back the same way. The ball has always been in your court. I hope you play it well, this time.

Pat: I've to go now Sheila. Just take your drama with you and go back to Paul. I'm sure both of you can find another toy to play with. Both of you are pathetic. Y'all fit and deserve each other. I'm working on filing for divorce so that you can have him to yourself, now that you are back full time with men.

Sheila: Please, let me explain myself, and if you still hate me, I promise, I'll leave you alone.

Pat: What about the videos?

Sheila: I have them. They will be ours. I mean yours, when you hear me out.

Pat: You've ten seconds, Sheila. Go!

Sheila: Thanks love.

Pat: Don't call me love. I hate you ass right now.

Sheila: I'm sorry. That is just how I feel.

Pat: You've five seconds left and counting . . .

Sheila: Please, allow me to read from my prepared text. I'm so sorry for what had transpired to-date. All I ever wanted was to know you and show you my undying love and genuine affection. Deep down, I feel you as the bank of a river feels the waves against it. Maybe I'm selfish to want you as much as I do; I found love in you that I know is real. The sort of love I always wanted. I want you to know me. I want you to find the best you deserve in me.

           Yes, I wanted you the first time I laid eyes on you. That was the day the city of Kope

announced you as the acting chief of police.
I fell in love with your beauty, intelligence,
and the professional way you carried yourself.
Later, I fell for your humility and how you
care for others (tears started to roll off her
cheeks). I would give all of me and all I've
to be with you. I agreed to join you and Paul
at your anniversary celebration so that I'd
be closer to you and hopefully be with you.
Looking back now, my approach was a big
mistake . . . I would've fought for you and
you only, until you would've me or reject me,
whichever you preferred.

Pat: Did it ever occur to you I may not feel the
same way about you?

Sheila: Please, hear me out. You promise.

Sheila stood and put on her jacket. She was feeling cold. She
then excused herself and went to the restroom. This time, she
was crying aloud.

While away, Pat called her office to cancel her ride back
home. "I hope she wasn't putting up a show this time," Pat
told herself.

"Your sister will be taking you home, Chief?" her security
guard asked. Yes, officer Deep, Pat responded. He has always
been a nosy and flirtatious officer . . .

Few times, Pat wanted officer Deep to do her when she was
lonely some early winter mornings. She just wasn't ready
to do the Hollywood hookups of movie stars fucking their
backup singers, bodyguards, or bouncers. At least for now, if
the truth be told, she was sexually starving but determined

to keep her legs closed as her mama taught her. She wished,
she doesn't have to listen to her mother in her time of need,
though.

Had it not been for one detail, Sargent Deep was her type: he
was tall, handsome with dark chocolate smooth skin, plump
lips, curly hair, presentable in simple clothing, gorgeous in
black tie, and a trophy of a man in jeans. He wears a thirteen
shoe size and possesses the most beautiful big brown long
hands. Above all, he seemed to have a big package between
his legs. There were few minor problems; officer Deep was
still obligated to one of his colleagues at work, Sargent Alice
Jeena Perez—they had her last son together. He also had two
sons with his former girlfriend, Sue Wilderbush. He lived
off again and on again with his current girlfriend, Maria,
a part-time nursing student and a full-time stripper on the
Boulevard leading to the navy yard.

"I can't go there now," Pat would tell herself after watching
Sargent Deep through her windows many evenings after her
evening bath before going to bed. She woke up a few times
with him on her mind . . . She once dreamt of him fucking
her in the limousine by the river, like a stranger in the night.

She once wanted to let him do her in one of their trips to
the quarterly police association meetings in San Francisco
but was afraid he wouldn't or couldn't keep a secret. As a
psychologist, she knew he couldn't be trusted. She knew his
kind: player, player . . .

On several occasions, during one of their unofficial chit-chat
in her garden, Sargent Deep had told her, over a bottle of
wine and fat free cheese with sautéed crab meat, about his
women conquests with a nonchalant attitude, as if he was
God's gift for all women with a pulse. Frankly, he was all that

and more—the Esquire Magazine's cover page type. Every woman would have accepted him as their private gift in any form presented. Pat had already concluded that fact the first time she laid eyes on him. That was one of the reasons she personally requested him to be her bodyguard. She had failed to do her research thoroughly on the life style of Sargent Deep. Loneliness and craven for hard dick had clouded her judgment.

"If he could tell me about his numerous affairs, God knows how many people he would tell if I let him fuck me," she concluded. She was right. Human resource records at police headquarters, showed that Sargent Deep was in high demand by many women in at least five different States of the union, evidenced by the child support payroll garnishments. He refuted many of the claims. "Until DNAs could be performed, all judgments for child support stand," his lawyer advised him.

Pat had painfully left him alone. Tomorrow is still another day, however.

———————————————•◦•———————————————

Pat had attended a couple of home-based sex toy parties. After a few self-help applications, she still preferred real assets possessed by male genders. In her present state of mind, however, Sheila was becoming more and more a better substitute.

Sheila returned from the restroom with changed attire. She had on a tight skirt and a white, tight, silk-blouse accentuating her perfect chest. She sat down, and continued her love expressions.

"Pat, I haven't had a normal sleep for a long time because of you. But that's my problem and not yours. I was sick for days when I learned that you'd been passed over for the chief of police in Kope. I wanted you to be with me and allow me to show you how I feel about you then. I wanted to take away your pains because I had experienced such pains. I know how to make you come alive. I did it once and I want you to let me do it again and forever."

She stood up again to go to the lady's room. She didn't want Pat to see her at her weak moments. Her mascara doesn't look good when she cries. She hated sniffing in public too. As she walked away, Pat could see her protruding butt stretching her tight skirt. Her two minutes' walk was mesmerizing and delicious . . . the rest of her body agreed.

To an observer, Sheila was sincere and speaking from her heart. She was genuine. She was truly in love. As a trained psycho analyst, Pat knew it too. "Shit, I'm in deep trouble. Maybe, I shouldn't have come here," Pat told herself.

"Excuse me Pat," Sheila said as she stood and went back to the bathroom. Everyone in their vicinity was now eyeing them and murmuring among themselves, "Are these people ok?"

The waitress crew, watching from afar, was also murmuring aloud among themselves about the embellished information they gathered from their co-server, Helena. They had not seen such two beautiful ladies in their restaurant. Definitely, not among the African Americans that patronized their restaurant, on a frequent basis, mostly after Sunday church services.

Pat immediately adjusted her blazer, fixed her hair, and followed Sheila to the bathroom.

With Pat's eyes also moist, she hugged Sheila and simply said, "Sheila, please drive me home."

"Are you sure?" Sheila asked.

"Yes, I'm sure unless you want me to change my mind," Pat replied. "What about your bodyguard," Sheila asked. "Never mind, I took care of him," Pat replied.

------------------------------•●•------------------------------

They drove in silence for a few miles before Pat said, "Sheila, you look amazing in your stripped green tank top."

"Thank you, Pat. You always look great in anything. I'm sure you look stunning in your officiating uniform. I would love to see you in it," Sheila returned the compliment.

Love in the air, by John Paul Young was playing in the back seat speakers. Pat smiled and watched Sheila as she drove, hoping nothing unexpected would happen.

CHAPTER 17

They arrived at Pat's gated community. "Go straight to the end of the street, watch out for the bumps, slow down after you go through the gate, and turn right after three blocks. My house is the fourth one on the right," Pat guided her.

Within minutes, they arrived at Pat's official two-story four-car garage residence. The state of Texas knew how to take care of its own—two full-time bodyguards, a chef, two full-time chauffeurs, two live-in maids, and a twenty-something year old maintenance, all muscle, college student from El-Salvador. Pat wouldn't mind sleeping with him too. Yes, the thought came to her mind many nights and a few times in the afternoon, when she came home for lunch.

Before Sheila could put her car into park, two hefty police officers approached her car with their guns drawn. "Heavens, here we go again. I'm going to jail now."

Pat looked into her eyes and softly said, "Relax, those are my security officers. They don't recognize your car. I've not announced your presence."

Sheila started shivering and appeared sick. She was in shock from her recent past experiences. She had been a little weak and fragile lately, mostly when agitated.

Pat beckoned to an officer and introduced Sheila. "Officer Bullhorn, this is Sheila, my sister visiting from Virginia. I think she isn't feeling well."

Pat and officer Bullhorn helped Sheila out of the car and walked her to the guest room adjacent to Pat's bedroom.

Officer Bullhorn would've preferred to carry Sheila by himself, on his shoulders, to his own bed, a few yards on the compound and nurture her to health. He really wanted to say, "I'll fuck her to good health."

Officer Bullhorn had his eyes full. The bouncing of Sheila's breasts in her green tight top was gratifying and made his job as a bodyguard/police officer, the best in the world. He wanted a piece of her. He wanted a taste of her. He was still standing by the door watching his boss and her sister from Mars until Pat said, "Thanks officer, we are ok now."

Pat guided Sheila to the loveseat and left the room for a cup of tea for her guest/sister.

"Pat, may I have also some crackers and cheese, please. I've not had a bite all day."

"Poor thing, I'll whip up something for you," Pat said as she walked towards the kitchen.

Within ten minutes, Pat brought a plate with thinly sliced whole-wheat beef sandwich with side orders of sliced pickles, strawberry, seedless red grapes, honey coated pecan, blue cheese, lettuce, baby spinach, sliced Oklahoma brand tomatoes, and freshly sliced Avocados. A glass of white wine also accompanied what could now be described as light late dinner. It was the same menu they'd ordered in one of their lunch dates in OldPort. The recipe was from Costa Rica. Pat just made few creative additions to it. She was artistic like that.

"Sheila, over there is the bathroom. You will find everything you need. I'll check up on you in a few," Pat said

"Won't you share the sandwich with me?" Sheila gently asked.

"Thanks, Sheila. I'm really not hungry. It's too late for me to eat anyway. I need to take a bath and take off these clothes I've had on all day. I feel dirty and uncomfortable," Pat replied.

Sheila didn't touch her wine. She drank orange juice and water instead.

Sheila, feeling sick or not, would have preferred to give Pat her bath. Even better, she wanted to take a bath with her and later relax with her together in her four-person Jacuzzi.

At the back of Sheila's mind, she remembered the lyrics; *it's getting hot in here* by Nelly. She was getting hot everywhere.

An hour later, Pat knocked at Sheila's door to check up on her and to bid her good night, reluctantly.

"Sheila, it's me. Is everything ok?"

"Yes, come on in, dear," Sheila replied.

Pat went in and simply said, "I just want to say good night and hope you're feeling better."

"I'm fine. Thank you for everything," Sheila said, as she sat in the middle of the bed, half naked, wishing she could

invite Pat to spend the night with her. She had prayed for
this night. As the adage goes, "Twenty years wasn't forever."
Her dreams that seemed twenty years in the making finally
arrived.

To her, plan C is producing results ahead of schedule, so far,
so good . . .

Pat gave Sheila a hug. On her way back to her room, Pat
could hear Sheila's iPhone playing the music of Whitney
Houston's best, *I'll always love you.*

Pat smiled, locked her door, and tried to go to bed. It had
been a long day. It would be a long sleepless night. Her
presumed lover for now, less than five feet away, was wide
awake next door. Her life was changing rapidly. She finally
accepted it.

The thought of Paul with Sheila suddenly overwhelmed her
and temporarily made her jealous and hateful to both of them.
She now wished she had been fucking Sargent Deep. She
would have gone to him, ten yards away or invited him to her
bedroom, to convince Sheila that she is involved with another
soul. It was too late. Her loneliness was exposed . . .

Within minutes, Pat found herself sobbing. She thought of
her life to-date and found it disturbing, empty, and unsettling.
In many ways, her life was unfulfilled, regardless of her
achieved status. Her public image was just that, image.

CHAPTER 18

Pat had achieved all she ever hoped for and more—she went
to a couple of top notch educational institutions. Will and
May Law was one of them. She had a loving family. She had
a manageable married life before the day of evil celebration
with Sheila. She was raised by both parents who had been
married for forty five years and lived in the same house they
built with their hands in the Mississippi Delta region. She had
everything she wanted. She achieved essentially all she ever
wished for. But there were holes in her perfect life. Most of
the holes were dug by her, however. She knew that much but
refused to accept any of her downside as her own creation.
She was human like the rest of the universe, incapable of
seeing their shortcomings.

She was married to a great man, Paul. She had pretended to
love him for the past fifteen years. Paul, on the other hand,
had loved and supported her unconditionally, in all her
endeavors. Looking back, she knew she had taken him for
granted. They did everything imaginable together as a loving
couple. At least, that was what Paul thought.

Paul was always proud of her. She was cautiously proud of
him. The circles of friends they kept were proud of them.
Friends and foes wanted to be like them. They presented
themselves well to their families, friends, and the public at
large. Many of their associates saw them as a perfect couple
and human beings created by God Almighty. Many spoke

about their perfect lives to family members and friends.
Even, a young pastor in their church mentioned their happy
marriage and their love for each other in his sermons on
Good-Friday. Her admirers forgot, however, that the grass is
always greener at the other side of the track.

She met her husband, at her ex-lover's wedding. She was an
uninvited guest. If truth be told, she ambushed her husband,
Paul on a rebound or something close to it. She wanted to
prove to her ex-lover that she too can find a man on her terms.
She was married five months later to Paul.

The ex-lover, whom she purposely invited to her own
wedding as a special guest of honor, refused to acknowledge
or attend her weeding. She had wanted to rub her new catch
in his face.

Paul had moved many times to distant places in support of
her careers. He was content with her even when she deprived
him of many of his wants and needs. He was smitten by her
beauty, grace, mannerism, great ethical habits, intelligence,
and most especially, her simplicity.

Paul was an ideal man. He was a progressive conservative.
He thought he had found his soul mate, and was smitten
by what he found. He forgot, however, that her beauty was
only skin deep. She was evil. She was a beautiful evil that
will draw any man to her den and devoured him without
any hesitation. He was ready to do for her all that may be
considered irrational in the eyes of those with the opportunity
to see her soul. No one ever saw her soul. In reality, she had
no soul . . .

In her world, which was the only world she cared about, made
her confortable to say, "Any man is a victim, if I want it so."

She always wanted everything her way since she was fourteen. She believed her ways will be the right and only way. To-date, she had failed in that line of thought.

She had an understanding husband who had never cheated on her until the night of February 5th, of which she was the chief planner, coordinator, and an active participant.

She had great jobs everyone would die for. She is currently the chief of police of one of the biggest cities in the country.

At the end of the day, she considered her life incomplete and unrewarding. All of a sudden, she found herself unhappy from within. All of a sudden she was sad, lonely, and unloved. All of a sudden, she came face to face with her shortcomings. At long last, she regretted the abortion she had while in college so that she could finish school without the burden of a baby. And when she decided to start a family, her doctor told her the only way she could conceive again was by artificial insemination. She refused that alternative—everything has to be her way, period.

She believed she would get pregnant the natural way, by the right man, blessed by the grace of God. Paul accepted her resolve when she told him without mincing words, "Paul, the only way I'll conceive is through natural processes."

She told him emphatically that her formula to motherhood was relatively simple:

Dick + vagina + sperm + womb + egg = A brown-eye boy.

She supported her self-evaluation and resolve by quoting Psalm 37:5, 7:

Commit everything you do to the Lord. Trust Him, and He will help you. Be still in the presence of the Lord, and wait patiently for Him to act.

She had been a devoted Christian all her life. Like many mothers in the scriptures, she believed she would be pregnant through God's intervention and blessing. She forgot one fact: Virgin Mary was the mother of Jesus Christ. Pat wasn't the Virgin Mary. She would never be. Thank God.

In her mind, if she failed to bear her husband children the natural way, it was because he was just an ordinary man and not the right man for her agenda. To-date, she wasn't convinced Paul is the chosen one.

All of a sudden, everything in her life was too late at the age of forty-something. All she had achieved to-date is naught except her big mansion—still listed for sale. What's more, she has a good job but barren, and her once devoted husband was doing everything under the sun to screw her sorority sister.

She was now lonely for the first time even though she had practically been lonely all her life. She felt guilty of how her life and actions of one night derailed her life. She was saddened the ways she had treated, over the years, everyone associated with her—her husband, friends, and family members.

She regretted her actions that led to the destruction of her high school boyfriend, Ted Samson. She never thought it was Christian or lady like to do what she did to get even with him. After all, he was her first true love. She loved him then and now. She will always be in love with him.

"What has come over me?" she asked herself. She wondered if she were bi-sexual or bi-curious. She has become a woman with many faces.

What's more, sleeping in the next room was Sheila, a lady she so much desired to comfort. The same lady she never thought she would be attracted to or wanted as a lover. She wanted to go to her and apologize for the pains she might have caused her. She wanted to go to her room, kiss her softly, hug her, and asked for her forgiveness, for destroying her family, even though, her family had been destroyed before they ever got together.

Unbeknownst to her, she was now sobbing aloud like a teenager under punishment, who had been confined to her room for the entire weekend without the social technology to communicate with her friends—the teenager had looked forward to spreading the news, in real time, about a "Slut" member of the cheerleading team caught, in broad daylight, giving blowjob to the heart throb football linebackers, Rodger, behind the bleacher.

Sheila couldn't sleep either. She heard Pat sniffing softly. She debated whether she should go and comfort her. Her love for Pat was no longer a game of conquest. It was for real.

Ten minutes later, Sheila was at Pat's door gently knocking and pleading, "Pat dear, please, let me in for a moment."

Pat opened the door with tears gushing down her cheeks like Niagara Falls. Sheila kissed her wet cheeks as if trying to lick all the tears away. She then hugged her gently and said, "Love, all will be ok. You will be fine. We would be fine. I'm here for you and you only. From now on, I'll take care of you."

Sheila changed Pat's tears-soaked pillow cases and gently laid her back to bed and tucked her under the cover. She went back to the kitchen to prepare a green tea with lemon and a teaspoon of honey for her. That was Pat's favorite beverage. She knew her so well. Little things like that gave Pat pause to reevaluate her disdain for Sheila.

Even under her current condition, Pat was exceptionally gorgeous—her skin was soft, silky, and warm. Her long dark hair spread neatly on her pillows. As she rested on her back, her breasts were perky and close to each other like two ripped and juicy melons picked at the right time, under the right climate. Her nipples were hard and pointed like the nipples of twenty-year old virgins from remote villages all over Africa, as they danced to the beat of talking drums, exhibiting their natural beauty to foreign dignitaries, in events organized by their own government, in the name of entertainment, tradition, and culture.

These African-naïve teenagers danced naked, all for free, under the illusion that they were pleasing their authorities, their parents, friends, villagers, and at the same time cherishing their beauty—their lips were full, their skins were clean, and chemical free. But at festival events, they were on display as commodities, as if waiting to be sold at a public auction. Maybe one day, these young innocent girls will be blessed by their gods to read Playboy Magazine and see how anyone in God's own country, United States of America, are paid a lot of dollars for showing even less beautiful skin and body parts, all in the name of freedom of expression and capitalism . . .

The more Sheila thought about Pat's beauty, the more she wished Paul was struck by a freight train or kidnapped by aliens so that he could be forgotten and out of their perfect union, forever. She has no patience. With prayers, her wish may come to pass in due time.

Five minutes later, Pat was resting on Sheila's chest, fast asleep, and snoring lightly from exhaustion. At the background, playing softly was Willie Nelson's best: *You are always on my mind.*

They were at peace. They were alone as it should have been the first time they met at their college sorority initiation.

To Sheila, life was joyous and peaceful the way she dreamt it. She knew she would die making Pat happy because her own happiness was irrelevant. It was true love she had for her. To-date, she couldn't explain why she loved Pat more than life itself. But again, she didn't want to think about all of that at the moment. She just wanted to savor the moment. She just wanted to guard over her dream lover like the angels of God guided over all of God's children.

CHAPTER 19

At exactly, 4:44am, Pat's official emergency red phone rang.
It was from the police headquarters. She was informed that
a probable homicide was under investigation at a glamorous
and exclusive downtown luxury hotel, where celebrities,
business executives, politicians, and professionals of the skin-
trade, gather for various reasons: business, personal, and
combination thereof.

Pat was also informed that her official secured car would be
waiting at her residence in fifteen minutes to bring her down
to the scene due to the sensitivity of the victim.

Pat gently slid away from Sheila. In less than ten minutes, she
was ready.

"Is everything ok," Sheila asked while still snuggling
peacefully under the cover.

"Everything is fine sweetie. Please go back to bed. I'll be
back in a few," Pat said. She kissed Sheila on her forehead.
As she was about to walk away, Sheila jumped of out of bed,
still naked, to give her a big hug and a kiss on her lips.

Sheila was in little heaven. "Finally, she called me Sweetie,"
She exuded happiness and renewed faith in her Lord, Jesus
Christ.

She couldn't go back to bed after Pat left. She went to the kitchen and started preparing breakfast. When breakfast was ready, she placed it on a warmer and went to take her shower. She rubbed her body with lavender oil from the Orient to make her skin soft and moist. She went to her travel bag and put on one of the sexy lingerie the stranger she met at Victoria's Secret bought for her. She looked through the window and counted the minutes Pat would be home . . . for breakfast and much more . . . finally, her ship had arrived. For someone who had waited for months to get to this moment, a minute was still like a thousand year.

It was a rainy morning but the sky was pleasant for the morning commuters. The rain made the driving slower than usual. Pat was anxious to reach her destination. She told her chauffer to speed it up a little. Her job has one drawback— 24-hour commitment. She hardly had any prolonged and unabridged private time or personal life. She really didn't need any private life under her circumstance.

Many thoughts ran through her mind and wondering who among the politicians was caught with his pants down and ended in tragedy.

"Female politicians are too smart to be caught with their pants down. But again, they wore skirts most of the time. It must be one of those male celebrities who were known for their reckless indiscretions," she concluded.

Less than two weeks ago, a famous local entertainer was rumored to have died of drug overdose at another famous downtown hotel, three miles east. His death was later classified as massive heart attack by the media outfit

controlled by his family. He was only 28. He left behind a
wife and six children from five different women. Also in
mourning were three girlfriends, his divorced mother (he
had just bought his mother a three bedroom condo in Miami
Beach), two sisters, a younger brother, and a 38-year old
mother of one of his former girlfriends who was rumored to
be heavy with his child—still pending was a request for a
DNA test by his family lawyer to ascertain the father of the
unborn child.

Upon Pat's arrival at the hotel, she was met at the door by the
fire Chief and the city Mayor.

"Good morning, Chief Peterman. How are you doing this
raining day?" the Mayor greeted her with a light hug.

"All is well, your honor," she replied.

The fire Chief beckoned Pat to a seat and then said, "Chief,
we think this incident is closer to home. We want you to
brave yourself when you identify the body."

"What body? Whose body? Which body? Was he or she
someone I knew?" These were some of the questions she was
asking herself aloud in rapid succession.

"My God, it must be Ted," she said aside.

She was nervous as she went through these questions again
and again in her mind. She checked-off all her acquaintances
she could remember, no one seemed to match her suspicion.
And again, she was convinced none of her friends near and
far, could afford to stay in such a talk-of-the-town-luxurious-
break-the-bank seven star hotel, anyway.

"Maybe, it was Ted." On second thought, she knew he couldn't afford to stay in such a hotel. "There is no way he could afford this place. He has no reason to be here. Maybe he was looking for his wife, Sheila. Maybe, he saw us together at the restaurant again," she said aside. "Lord, don't let it be Ted," she prayed.

All of a sudden, Pat became light headed. Her heart was racing faster than normal. For a brief moment, she saw stars as in a quiet night. She saw Sirius descending at the horizon as if the day of Armageddon had finally arrived. She had seen many deaths in her line of business; her feeling on this one was different.

The Mayor walked side by side with her while making irrelevant chit-chat to kill the time before they got to the victim. The two minutes' walk seemed like eternity.

The hotel manager welcomed them and opened the door adjacent to the hospitality room where the deceased laid and surrounded by paramedics who had tried effortlessly to revive him.

"The hotel staff had found the victim in his own pool of blood in the maintenance staff bathroom, adjacent to the hospitality room, at exactly 3:42 am," the hotel manager said.

Pat lifted the white sheet over the victim's face, viewed the corpse, and announced, "Sweet Moses, he is Mr. Paul Peterman, my husband of sixteen years."

The Mayor held her up from falling. Her mind and existence evaporated. Like a tigress, however, she composed herself and thanked all present for their efforts. She couldn't even shed tears. She accepted her husband's wristwatch and a purported suicide note, drenched in his pool of blood. The gun, still clutched in his hand, was collected by the police as evidence.

On her way home, she read the short blood-soaked note. She knew it was written with her husband's hand writing. It simply said, "I died for the two I love."

Pat's interpretation: he died for me and Sheila . . .

As Pat started to cry, she went over in her mind, the beginning of the end: February 5th, "A date which will live in infamy." According to her record, that was the day the love she shared with her husband officially took the wrong turn, and for all practical purposed ended.

When she got home, she went straight to one of her guest rooms and locked the door. Within minutes, she started crying uncontrollably.

Looking back, she should have loved her husband as a loving wife before it was too late. She now realized how she had taken his life and the lives of many around him for granted . . .

Sheila, who was still in Pat's room, had seen her as she drove up through the window. She quickly covered herself with a white silk bed sheet over her lingerie, went to the guest room, and started to pound on the door asking her to let her in. She wanted to find out what was the matter.

Pat's chauffer and bodyguard who were privileged to the events of the day went upstairs and told Sheila, "Madam, Chief Peterman had just found out that her husband passed away this morning at the airport hotel here in Warsaw."

Sheila sank into the cushioned bench in the corridor and began to weep, and shouting, "Why? Why? Why Paul? My gracious Lord, why him?"

Strangely as it may sound, she loved Paul too. Paul was a great provider, unselfish, caring, soft spoken, and willing to please her even at his own expense. She loved his pleasurable long hard dick even when she pretended not to want it. She knew he loved her. In a way, she loved him on a selective and limited basis. Everyone that knew him loved him. He was simply a good man.

Paul was a man who wanted to love and be loved because both had eluded him most of his life. He was a private man in search of a loving family and peace of mind. He never knew his mother and was raised by a loving stepmother. He ran away from home at the age of fifteen in search of success, in the big city, before he joined the military at eighteen or nineteen. He never discussed his past in details with anyone, even with his wife, because he wanted to move forward and leave his past behind.

On his thirty-ninth birthday, he retired from the army with full benefits. Before his death, he was the CEO of his international construction company, with offices in two states and three foreign offices in St. Martin, Haiti, and Jamaica. Costa Rica is slated for another potential office in three years to meet the growing demand from middle class African American professionals vacationing in that part of the world.

For the first time, Sheila and Pat shared a common tragedy. To one, the tragedy was from a selfish game. To the other, it was the end of love that never existed.

"I'll be out in a sec," Pat told Sheila behind closed door.

Moments later, Pat went to her bedroom where Sheila was standing nervously. She had been crying too. Pat sat down at the edge of the bed but immediately stood and sat on the ottoman besides a loveseat to keep her distance from Sheila. She wiped her face with the back of her palms, cleared her throat, and said:

> *Sheila, as you might have heard, Paul killed himself this morning. My life has come full circle.*
>
> *My life is finished now. Sheila, you can't hurt me anymore. You can't hurt Paul anymore. You can't hurt us anymore. In fact, no one can hurt us anymore. No one in this freaking world could do anything to us now. I can't hurt him anymore. It doesn't matter any longer who is to blame. I might as well consider myself dead. Or what else is left for me?*

She started crying profusely and then continued with a true sense of loss for the first time in her life:

> *Paul loved me. Our love might not be perfect but it was the best love we shared. We did what we agreed to do for love and nothing else. Sheila, I'll not judge you because I'll leave that to the Lord Almighty.*

Pat picked up the Bible from the bed stand and read aloud
Luke 6:37, 41:

> *Do not judge and thou shall not be judged. Do
> not condemn, and you will not be condemned.
> Forgive, and you will be forgiven.*
>
> *Why do you look at the speck of sawdust in
> your brother's eye and pay no attention to the
> plank in your own eye?*

"Here are the DVDs you gave me. You can add them to the
collections you gave to Paul about your affairs with him. You
can do whatever you want with them. Nothing matters to me
now. Sheila, may God have mercy on our soul . . . I will be
taking my husband's remains back to OldPort for burial in
a few days. I hope you will consider me just as dead in your
life, too."

Sheila attempted to interject and said, "Pat, I'm so sorry
and . . . ," but Pat, in a cool and calculated manner stood and
left the room. She was finally done with her.

CHAPTER 20

All Sheila wanted to say, if Pat had given her the chance was:

> *Pat, I'm so sorry beyond words. I never thought it will end this way for Paul. I never believed he loved me beyond . . . There is no need to trample on the dead but I never wanted him. Not the way he wanted me. I told him so, countless times, and he just wouldn't have any of it. To me, it was history repeating itself once again in my life. No one ever wanted me to be me.*

Then, she narrated the summary of her life for everyone who has ears to hear:

"I was the last child of three girls, born to a loving parent from the deep-south, 39 years ago. I dropped out of college in my freshman year to pursue modeling. My mother later enrolled at a community college in order to encourage me to go back to school. She wanted to show me her support and to prove that if she could go to school at her age, I've no reason to drop out. Her strategy worked. I later completed college in two and a half years later. Subsequently, I obtained my MBA and a CPA license from the great state of Mississippi.

To this day, I never knew my father. My mother always told me, he died in the Long K war. She loved me and trained me to work hard, study hard, and respect my elders. She taught me how to be independent and equally care for mankind. My upbringing was not easy, but I will not trade it for anything in this world. My past built my character and prepared me to cope with my present and my future.

My mother never knew my sexual orientation. Even though I talked with her about many other things, I was still ashamed to confide in her my real sexual identity. Maybe she would've understood but I'm not ready or willing to take that chance. To this day, I never told her about what many called the *demon within me*. Maybe when I meet my maker, I'll ask the Almighty why I am what I'm. I'll wait for His judgment and not the judgment of any man, woman, government, or religious stewards.

I was never attracted to or wanted to be with men but Ted convinced me otherwise. I agreed to marry him because until recently, I wanted to hide my sexual preference and please my mother at the same time. I gave him two lovely children I never wanted.

I never loved Ted the way a wife should love her husband, no matter how much he tried to show me his brand of love. History seemed to have repeated itself in my life one more time. I asked Ted for a divorce many times, he refused. I cheated on him openly with his consent, and yet, he still refused to let me go. The ex-girlfriend I left for him in college is now married to one of my ex-girlfriend, Deena T., in the great state of Massachusetts, with two adopted girls and one of their own, conceived by artificial insemination. They announced the adoption and the birth of their son on Twitter and Facebook. From their latest update on Facebook, they seemed happy. Such happiness is never within my reach. Lord, help me, for I'm lost and empty.

For nearly two years, Ted allowed my girlfriends to stay with me as I wanted, when I wanted, and as long as I wanted. He accommodated me in other to keep me on the leash and thus forced me to stay with him.

Our children simply knew my lovers as *Aunt Sherry, Niece Joyce, Dr. Niki, attorney Underwood, godmother Harris, co-worker Traycy, hairdresser Freshbush, or babysitter Clara."*

Sheila began to cry but continued:

"Ted cried silently many nights when I slept with any of my girlfriends in the guest room or in my daughter's bedroom. Ted never participated. He never wanted any part of it. He hated my life style but subjected himself to it for the sake of our children's dignity and his dignity. He wanted to avoid public humiliation my life style might bring to him, his friends, and his family, if any of it becomes public.

I was unhappy. He was unhappy. Looking back now, we were never happy together. He dragged me to his pastor several times so that he could pray over me asking the Lord to 'Take out the Lucifer in me.' His pastor failed to make me born again, and until this day, hated me for refusing to sleep with him.

I regret my existence. I failed myself as I failed Ted. I failed my mother as I failed those that probably loved me without the knowledge of who I am. I failed Ted as I had failed my children. And God knows, I might have also contributed to the demise of Paul. I failed him too. Pat, I had failed you as well.

Paul and I spoke at length about his life. He genuinely opened up to me because he felt at peace with me as he hadn't felt for a long time. We spoke about him mostly at dinner table, many times, about what he would do if he could be with me exclusively. I listened to him as much as I could. Several times, I tuned him out and refused to listen to him. He confessed to me that I was his only hope. Like my husband, Ted, I told him, he was not the type I wanted. He tried to convince me otherwise. He promised he'll do anything under the sun to take away my pains, if I would only give myself a chance to love him, even just for a spell. I told him countless times that I had tried that scenario many times and failed.

"Many had tried it before you and failed, Paul, I told him each time we were together." I was rude to him intentionally so that he would let me move on. I know he loved me. I wanted to frustrate him, hopefully, he will hate me enough to leave me alone . . . I took advantage of him . . . I used him at his expense. I'm sorry, Paul . . .

I'll forever ask for his forgiveness. I never meant for any of it to happen. I was only looking for love. I want my own love to be my own brand of love without looking over my shoulders. I was sick of running away from my inner being. I was tired of the pains from within . . . even though I couldn't be what many wanted me to be. What I'm and become are beyond my control. Lord, please help me.

Finally, I can now confess in the presence of my Lord the beginning of the end:

I knew all about Pat's letters, gifts, cards, and invitations, to my husband. Many of the letters were addressed, in care of me. I didn't react to any of them the ways Pat expected. I knew she wanted Ted by any means, the same way I wanted Ted to leave me alone. In my mind, I wanted Ted to go back to Pat, his high school sweetheart, so that I could force him to give me a divorce. I was more than ready to oblige him at any time. I knew about Pat's secret taping and bugging of our house two weeks after it started. I was able to view the videos of all her taping in my house, including my affairs with my girlfriends and more. For heaven's sake, I'm still the head of forensic technologies at my firm. In fact, the idea to contact Pat and make her fall in love with me started the day I discover the bug in our living room.

I wanted to test my theory that if Pat wanted my husband, then I must do all within my power to make her fall in love with me. Quid pro quo—her beauty also helped my cause. I knew Ted didn't want her for my sake, for the sake of her betrayer to him, which gave me the opportunity to set in motion my own agenda. I planned to destroy her life the same way she wanted to destroy mine and my family, even though I have no family to speak of. Unbeknownst to her, I'm a lesbian, ready and willing to fly away from a man I never loved. That was how the destructive game started, if I can describe the whole episode as such. After five years of The Game, I fell in love with her. The rest is now history . . . Lord, forgive me, for I have sinned."

Sheila was in a daze. Her future was in doubt. All of a sudden, her existence had no meaning.

Less than an hour later, she walked slowly but majestically to her car. All Pat's household staff could say to her was, "Ms. Sheila, we hope everything is ok. Is the Chief ok?" She didn't answer. They had no clue, the extent of her pains . . .

She drove around town aimlessly for hours before going to her hotel to fly back home.

She was briefly questioned by the hotel security and let go after obtaining her personal information. Like Pat, she did not know what the future has in store for her.

She had lost Pat—the love she thought belonged to her by all means necessary. One of the necessary means had now taken his life and possibly destroyed the lives of many others, including that of his wife.

The only and last time Pat saw Sheila after the Warsaw encounters was at the funeral church service for her husband, Mr. Paul Benjamin G. Peterman, deceased.

CHAPTER 21

Sheila sent to the funeral home assorted floral arrangements for the remembrance of the deceased, Mr. Paul B.G. Peterman, alias Puky, as he lay in state, the following:

- Twenty four yellow roses from Paul's great State of New York.
- A bouquet of Bluebonnet with seventeen bulbs to represent Pat's great lone star state of Texas.

At the middle of the funeral church service, Sheila walked in, dressed in white slacks, a black V shaped blouse, leopard stiletto, a red purse, a dark sunshade, and a white hat. She appeared like an angel temporarily visiting from the heavens, as the church choir was singing, "Hallelujah" composed by Ludwig Van Beethoven.

She walked up to Paul's casket, knelt down beside it, and prayed silently for nearly five minutes for everyone present to witness.

Pat did her best to avoid her and her drama. She admitted Sheila was fine and well put together.

Sheila then placed over Paul's casket a single long stemmed mountain laurel flower from "Intercourse," representing her own great state of Pennsylvania.

It had now become clear why Sheila loved intercourse so much. She was born in the little town called "Intercourse," in Pennsylvania.

With that, she had given Paul 42 flowers to accompany him as he finally ascended to the right hand of his Lord, Jesus Christ. Paul had died at the age of 42 for love or the lack of it.

She got up, turned around, walked towards Pat, and gave her a hug. She also gave her a small CD box containing all of her illegal taping. It was marked, "Shattered disks, shattered hearts."

She whispered in Pat's ear, this time without tears, without fear, without regrets, and said, "I will always love you. Good bye. I consider myself dead too."

As she was walking away towards the exit door, the choir was singing the song she had requested from the funeral choir director for the occasion, "God be with you, until we meet again," from 2 Corinthians 1:2, with the lyrics by Jeremiah E Rankin. She had promised the choir director a diner date, for his cooperation . . .

Her eyes were full of tears. She looked up into the heavens, with both hands in the air, as every mourner in attendance, including Chief, Mrs. Patricia C. Peterman, Esq., stood up by protocol, and joined her in reciting aloud, Psalm 23:

> *The Lord is my shepherd,*
> *I shall not want.*
> *He makes me to lie down in green pastures;*
> *He leads me beside the still waters.*
> *He restores my soul;*
> *He leads me in the paths of righteousness for*
> *His name's sake.*

Yea, though I walk through the valley of the
shadow of death,
I will fear no evil;
For you are with me;
Your rod and your staff, they comfort me.
You prepare a table before me in the presence
of my enemies; you anoint my head with oil;
My cup runs over.
Surely goodness and mercy shall follow me
All the days of my life;
And I will dwell in the house of the Lord forever.

Sheila then disappeared as she had appeared.

Even Reverend T. S. Sunshine, the officiating paid Pastor of
the funeral service, stopped in the middle of his sermon to
wonder who in sweet Jesus, Sheila might be. Sheila wasn't
mentioned anywhere in the funeral service program.

CHAPTER 22

After the funeral services, Pat went home to receive condolences from well-wishers including close friends, former colleagues, and family members. People she hadn't met, who had admired her from afar, stopped by to express their condolences. The death of her husband opened the flood gate of visitors from those who wanted her in their dreams.

She also wanted to spruce up her house and make it available for sale with another aggressive real estate agent, at a substantial reduced price. She was open to any offers, including owner-financing. She also wanted a closure.

The mayor, her former friend/employer, was among the well-wishers. The mayor was ahead in the poll in his gubernatorial race after Pat's positive testimony about his public park's sexual indiscretions. They had always kept in touch. The mayor advised her to reconsider selling her home until after the election because he has big plans for her in his administration.

Sheila had stopped by on her way from the funeral service to drop her copy of their house keys. She wanted closure too.

Theodore Samson, the estranged husband of Sheila, Pat's high school lover, stopped by to express his condolences. He looked asinine, pathetic, but genuinely concerned. For the first time without being asked, he apologized to Pat for everything in their past. He was intoxicated by the time he arrived at Pat's Mansion.

He recounted the circumstance that ended their relationship twenty years ago. He finally confessed his affairs with Pat's twin sister and not with the twenty-year old community college student he purportedly confessed to, in his letter. He admitted to all the load of lies that followed. He regretted and accepted Pat's twin sister's abortion as his responsibility. He apologized and asked for forgiveness for the hurt he might have caused her.

Without hesitation, he told her, "Boobsy, I'll always love you. You had asked for my forgiveness. I came here today to say, I forgive you with all my heart. I wish we could do it all over. I hope you will forgive me too. We had both suffered enough."

Throughout his confession, Pat was crying nonstop. However, before she could summon the courage to respond, Ted stood and wondered off aimlessly into the night as he had been doing lately, repeating the words of Jesus Christ on the cross, "Lord, why have thou forsaken me?"

Pat wanted to move on. In a sense, the third chapter of her life was coming to an end.

———————•●•———————

Two days after the funeral services, two detectives paid Pat a visit for some preliminary fact-findings surrounding the death of her husband at the Warsaw Airport International Hotel. They were representing the hotel homicide division for insurance purposes, among other things. Mrs. Sheila Samson would be next on their agenda, once they could locate her whereabouts.

The two detectives expressed their sadness for the death of Pat's husband and wished her the best life could offer, under the circumstances.

The first detective respectfully informed Pat she was not considered a suspect to the demise of her husband at the present time. They informed her that they had read her husband's short suicide note. They also informed Pat that she didn't have to answer any of their questions, if she decided not to.

Of course, Pat was a lawyer, and was aware of her rights; she had no reason to invoke the Fifth Amendment, at least, not yet.

"Gentlemen, please have a seat while I arrange some refreshments," she told the detectives.

The lead detective (detective #1) extended his condolences to Pat once again. The two detectives, in turn, described in details the information gathered about her husband since they believed he arrived at the hotel, the evening before the day of his demise, and the narratives from people of interest surrounding his suicide. They made it known to her that other detectives are currently searching for the Nigerian cab driver that brought him to the hotel from the gun shop where he purchased the gun he used to kill himself. They confirmed that they had interrogated the Haitian hotel bellboy her husband spoke with about a lady guest he was meeting at the hotel for dinner, at approximately 6:45pm. The bellboy was the fellow that took his bag to hotel room 555-C1, and had testified, under oath, that the occupant refused to open the door and only spoke with the hotel's night manager behind closed door. The time was 6:56pm.

Pat was also informed that the husky gun dealer where her husband purchased the Glock pistol found on him had verified the day, time, and cost of purchase. Furthermore, the bullet from the gun matched the bullet that shattered his right ventricle. According to the medical examiner, "His cause of death was self-inflicted wound with the estimated time of death, 3:42 am."

"He listed you, Chief Peterman, as his wife and your address as his permanent residence on the bill of sale," the second detective interjected.

Pat's only response was, "Really?"

Detective #1:	Chief Peterman, were you aware your husband, Mr. Peterman was coming to Warsaw on or before the day of the tragedy?
Pat:	No sir.
Detective #1:	Do you know of any reasons Mr. Peterman would be at the hotel the day preceding his death?
Pat:	No sir.
Detective #1:	Do you know of any reason Mr. Peterman lodged at the same hotel with your sister?
Pat:	My sister?
Detective #2:	I beg your pardon, I mean, Mrs. Sheila Samson.
Pat:	Oh no. I wasn't aware of that.

Detective #2:	Did you know his last phone call was made to your sister? I beg your pardon, Mrs. Sheila Samson.
Pat:	I didn't know that sir.
Detective #1:	Were you and your husband having any marital or financial problems?
Pat:	Not much different from any other couple in a long-term marriage.
Detective #1:	Do you know of any reason your husband didn't stay in your residence this last trip, as he had done numerous times in recent past?
Pat:	I don't know the reason sir.
Detective #1:	Did you know your sister has used the same hotel, stayed in the same room, at least once in the last fifteen days with your husband?
Pat:	Wow. No sir.
Detective #2:	Do you know that your husband paid cash to register for his lodging at the hotel under a fictitious name, Pulyn Samson, this time around?
Pat:	I didn't even know he was in town.
Detective #2:	Do you know of any reason your husband didn't bring with him a single article of clothing when he checked into the hotel?
Pat:	No sir.

Detective#1:   Chief Peterman, do you recognize this article of clothing?

Pat: They are mine, I think.

Detective #2:   Ok then. Do you know the reason your sister, Mrs. Samson, checked out of the hotel the same day Mr. Peterman committed suicide and left behind in her hotel room a blue shopping bag containing your article of clothing?

Pat: Of course not.

Detective #1:   Do you have any explanations as to why your husband and your sister shared the same room at the hotel a few times in the past?

Pat: I wasn't even aware they had been in town together.

Detective #1:   Are you saying you knew one of them was in town and not the other?

Pat: I didn't say that sir. I only knew Mrs. Samson was in town the evening before my husband's suicide.

Detective #1:   Do you know that your husband was caught on the hotel security camera trying to force his way into your sister's room minutes after she complained to the hotel night manager and asked the manager to, and I quote, "Keep the SOB away from me?"

Pat: Of course not.

Detective #2:   Were you close to your sister?

Pat: Who?

Detective #1:   I beg your pardon, I meant, Mrs. Sheila Samson, Chief.

Pat: Yes, a little

Detective #1:   How close, Chief?

Pat: Like I said, a little.

Detective #2:   Did you have a dinner date with your sister the evening before the tragedy?

Pat: Yes. We had dinner at the "Licking Good" café on 39th and Lee Street.

Detective #2:   I thought you said, you knew her just a little?

Pat: We actually reconnected recently in OldPort, before I moved down here.

Detective #2:   What happened after the dinner date?

Pat: We went home together.

Detective #2:   By home, you meant your official residence?

Pat: Yes detective.

Detective #1:   Did she discuss her encounters with your husband at her hotel?

Pat: No sir.

Detective #1: Did you discuss with your sister the problems you're having with your husband at any time during the evening you were together or at any other time?

Pat: Of course not.

Detective #2: Did your sister discuss with you the frictions between her and your husband?

Pat: No. Remember, I didn't know my husband was in town.

Detective #1: Ok, I'm going to ask you straight up then, do you think your sister and your husband were having an affair?

Pat: Detective, your guess is as good as mine.

Detective #1: Do you know the two people your husband said he died for in his suicide note?

Pat: Me and my sister . . . I mean Mrs. Samson, I guess . . .

Detective #1: Were you aware that two hours ago, your sister's car was found abandoned at the entrance to the CB Bridge, and a motorist saw a lady, fitting her description, walking away from her vehicle towards the edge of the bridge?

Pat: Not at all. I mean, no.

Detective #1: Chief, here is another note we found in your sister's hotel room with your husband's belongings. Do you recognize the handwriting?

Pat: Can I take a look at that, please?

Detective #2:   Here you go, Chief.

Pat: Yes. It's my husband's.

Detective #1:   Are you certain?

Pat: Yes sir. I was married to him for nearly sixteen years.

Detective #1:   Do you want us to read you the note's contents?

Pat: Sure, go ahead, please.

Detective #2:   Chief, I'm quoting your husband here. "Love, please don't do anything to hurt our baby. I know you have little love or passion for me. I realize that we love and share the same woman. The baby in your womb belongs to me. The baby belongs to love and for whatever rational reasons, belongs to us to cherish. The baby completes me. Please, don't hurt the baby. That's part of me growing inside of you. That is my life. That's all I have left. That is all I'll ever have left. Don't hurt the baby, I beg you in the name of God. You know Pat never loved me enough to give me even a child. I would die for you and the baby . . .

Detective #1:   Do you know the woman your husband and sister shared?

Pat: Pregnant at 39? After two grown up children? I think I heard enough. Please, stop . . .

Detective #1: Please, answer the question.

Pat: I don't know.

Detective #1: We found her medical report and the sonogram's result in her abandoned car. It's a boy!

Pat: Could I take a look at that, please?

Detective#1: Yes, you can. You and your sister are beautiful and almost look alike. Are you twins?

Pat: Thanks. She is actually my soror sista.

Detective #1: We thought as much. Mrs. Peterman, we're about done here, Chief. One more question. As we speak, were you aware the divers from the search and rescue team from the VB community emergency squad are combing the area and the surrounding waters for the person purported to have walked away from an abandoned car with a registered Virginia license plate number "Sheila-PP?"

Detective #2: I think we know the two people your husband died for now.

Pat: Gentlemen, I must stop the interview at this point.

At this juncture, Chief Patricia Peterman requested an end to the interview because she would like to consult with her lawyer before answering any further questions. Thank God, she was not under oath. All her affairs and lies seem to be coming alive and colliding at a speed faster than the speed of light.

For the first time in months, she walked to the liquor cabinet and poured herself three-finger of dark Jamaica rum with orange juice, tonic water, and a dash of cranberry, to cool her nerves.

She offered the detectives the same, they refused with gratitude. They don't drink in the presence of suspects . . .

After expressing their condolences, once again, the two detectives left Chief Patricia Peterman, until they will meet again.

She bade the detectives a good day and walked back to her den.

Detective #2 commented on their way out, "That's one fine mama. Her husband must be mental to have killed himself for another woman." The second detective then added, "Amen." Obviously, they hadn't met Sheila.

Half intoxicated; Pat blamed herself for all events that destroyed her life and many others. She was distraught, betrayed, and saddened.

CHAPTER 23

After 20 years, Pat's therapy finally made her face her own demon. She could now confess the truth about Ted in one sentence: "Ted never raped me." She exaggerated the rape encounter to make a point that no means no. She also wanted to save face with her parents who had told her to be home before 11:00 pm. It was two o'clock in the morning when she cried rape. Yes, Ted wanted to make love to her that warm morning, and not as she described the whole affair in her rape complaint to the police and the Korean-American convenience store entrepreneurs.

Most importantly, she was really pissed off with Ted for denying ever sleeping with her twin sister, Disaya. He swore on his mother's life and said, "I knew her not." Ted never thought she knew. Ted's so-called friends, who were looking for sympathy fuck, had told her all about the affairs. She just wanted the truth. She would've have forgiven him, only if he had just confessed.

Disaya had already confessed to Pat about one affair the day Pat scolded her in jealousy, asking her to stop flirting with Ted and clean up her school grades.

"You're not giving up the booty to Ted anyway," Disaya told Pat out of spike.

"You're not Sammy's type. Stop throwing yourself at him," Pat fired back.

"FYI, he's good too," Disaya told her as she was walking away to Ted's baseball game.

Everyone in their family was ashamed to discuss Disaya and her loose ways. They knew Disaya slept around but didn't want to believe Ted was responsible for her pregnancy. Disaya later performed an abortion, moved to Afghanistan, and worked at a Catholic mission. She was willing to risk her life in a war zone, to get away from her past, present, and probably her future. She was in a do or die relocation mission because nothing tangible was working her way so far. She had lost the love of her twin sister and nothing else matters.

Even though Pat wanted to punish Ted for sleeping with her sister, she never thought her mother would take the rape charge that far. She was only eighteen, naïve, and took all her TV sex education programs on "No means no" at face value. She would have forgiven him because to this day, she loved him.

All she ever wanted from Sammy (Ted's nickname) was a true confession and an apology. She thought, if the medical examiner had done her job, she would have known there was no medical evidence of rape. At the tender age of eighteen, she never knew authorities in her part of the world, didn't give a damn about black chic.

She lied to the police about the rape and everything else that she said that night. She was relieved; however, Sammy didn't go to jail.

Pat had followed Sammy's careers while he was in the military and beyond. She had all the clippings of all local newspaper's reports about him, including his military service, and civilian achievements. She adored him in uniform, most especially. Countless times, she wanted to go to him and apologize. She suffered in silence because of what her family and friends would say. After all, her family had moved back to Mississippi to erase Ted's memory forever. They warned her to stay away from the two-faced son-of-a-bitch-mother-fucker Satan. Yes, they hated him with every ounce of blood in their veins. They wanted his name erased from their memories, all based on false information provided by their beloved pretty and innocent daughter, Pamela, a.k.a Pat.

She knew about Sheila. She followed her career too. She was present the day Ted and Sheila got married. It was at that event she met her husband, Paul. She followed their children's birthdays. She wished their children had belonged to her and Ted as a couple. She wanted to share the air Ted breathed.

She had the surveillance reports on how many pairs of shoes Ted had and where he kept his favorite silver and white boxers with the impressions of Taylor Swift's glossy red lips. She had on tape, his once-a—month sex with his wife, always in the bathroom. Sheila always took her shower immediately after their sex act.

She had on tape, the day Ted prepared dinner for three, to celebrate the birthday of two of Sheila's girlfriends and then played the roles of chef and butler for his wife and her acquaintances—Sheila called them Milk and Sugar. She knew Ted slept alone that night and Milk and Sugar spent the night with Sheila. At one point, she knew what he had for breakfast on his birthdays. Her secret manifesto about him had documented five years of his birthday's activities. In her spare times, she had viewed Sheila's sex acts with her girlfriend on videos. A few times, she had watched them live! She hated watching the God-forsaken acts in real time.

She knew about Sheila's lesbianism. In her judgment, she knew she isn't bi-sexual. She knew about all her girlfriends for the past five years and Ted's consent to them. She knew every time Sheila's girlfriends stayed in their house and for how long. She knew their names, their profession, and their places of work. She knew one or two of her girlfriends were self-employed—one was a hairdresser. She knew at least one that was married. She knew another was a stripper in the most dangerous part of town. She particularly knew about a tall, skinny, flat chested, chocolate beautiful girlfriend, who lost custody of her daughter because of alleged child neglect and endangerment. She saw to the arrest debacle and was a catalyst to the charges filed against her. Thanks to her friends at the city hall, in the department of child support services.

She knew one of Sheila's girlfriends, Anna-Maria, who also worked in the same building with her as an assistant accounts payable clerk in the finance department, on the seventh floor of the public safety building. She saw her practically every day. She wanted to get her fired but unsuccessful . . . public employees' union made that impossible.

After all, Sheila was her sorority sister. She kept tab on her 24/7. For heaven's sake, Pat was the acting chief of police of a city with total population of less than 400,789, United States' citizens included.

She kept tab practically on everyone of interest in town. She had her own secret, semi-mini FBI files on anyone she wanted. So far, Ted was her primary target and suspect. In fact, ninety percent of her secret files contained only Ted and his family affairs.

Yes, she knew all about the legal mumbo jumbo of invasion of privacy. She was schooled about, and on illegal wiretaps. And, yes, she knew all about illegal entry. None of them matters, when it comes to Ted. After all, she wasn't the President of the United States of America who has to worry about explaining to the whole world, especially to the naïve 18-28-year old citizens, why it's necessary to snoop on all Americans . . .

To this day, the files on the family affairs of Theodore Samson were marked "CLASSIFIED" since he, Ted, was captured on national television protesting against the Iraq war while in uniform, when it was illegal for him to do so as a reserve intelligence marine officer—he has one of the highest security clearances in his line of work.

From that day forward, she had the opportunity to make Ted her subject of interest, in the name of national security.

To her, the American Civil Liberties Union can go to hell with their lawsuits and advocate for civil rights and privacy, under the rule of law . . . To her, half of the populations is ordinary and thus inconsequential.

She once told a friend during dinner, "What the hell is the rule of law when I have cause?" The friend, a lawyer by trade, asked her with absolute sense of concern, "Can you do all that?" Pat looked squarely into her eyes and quoted the famous phrases of an American President, "Yes, I can. Yes, we can."

In her dictionary, when it came to Ted, freedom of speech didn't exist. To her, privacy wasn't a word, not when it applies to Sammy, her only love, who refused to confess his sins, and asked for her forgiveness, so that they can be together as she planned.

Finally, she admitted that she had sinned against everyone she ever knew and her Lord Jesus Christ.

"None of these should've happened on my watch," she said
aloud, as she walked to her closet to change her clothes
for the evening before going to bed. She was lonely from
within . . .

She started sobbing like a ten-year old freckle-face boy
grounded for misbehaving at grandma's dinner table
on Easter Sunday. February 5th was the day she would
remember for the rest of her life. She blamed herself for
contributing to the death of her husband, Paul. She blamed
herself for her inability to bear him offspring when she had
the time and opportunity to do so.

She wanted to blame him for abandoning her with all her
faults which he had endured for almost sixteen years. She
regretted accepting her current job. Maybe, if she hadn't
moved away and instead stayed with her husband in OldPort,
her life might have been different; and Paul might still be
alive. And again, she knew it was too late to blame the
deceased. "What was done had been done," she told herself.
Blaming herself was also too late.

She understood at the late hour, her husband's reason for
wanting and loving Sheila. Yes, her husband was wrong by
the norm of society for continuing his adulterous relationship
with Sheila, after February 5. Nonetheless, she understood
his reasoning even though she denounced his resolve. After
all, she was a willing participant and a catalyst to the whole
wedding anniversary affair.

All of a sudden, she found her true inner soul and admitted
that when all was said and done, she had misfired by her
ideology of life. Her ambition had blinded the most important
thing in her life: to love and be loved by the only man who
blindly loved her with all her faults. Her selfishness had
beclouded her appreciation for decency and respect.

She wanted to blame Sheila for all the havoc she did to derail her manageable marriage. She finally accepted she was partially responsible for the mayhem that caused Sheila's husband, Ted, to be considered mentally imbalance.

Among the gang of four, Paul, Pat, Sheila, and Ted; only Paul was innocent and a victim because Pat had used Sheila and the wedding anniversary stunt to get to Ted, just as Sheila had used Paul to get to her, which ultimately got rid of her husband, Ted.

She had lied to Paul all these years about her true love for him. She never told him about the purported rape, until the issue came to light in her deposition against Ted. She never told him the reason she never enjoyed love making with him. It was very simple: Paul wasn't Ted.

With tears, she acknowledged to herself why she never wanted to have children for him—he would not be the right father for her children. She wanted her first love, Ted, to be the father of her children. She felt guilty that she waited too long, for selfish reasons, and allowed Sheila to take her rightful place with Ted. She regretted marrying Paul just to be closer to Ted. She confessed now that she had married Paul out of revenge, and to show Ted that she too can find someone who would love her just as much. She was wrong.

She had moved back to OldPort hoping and determined to start her life all over with Ted whenever he is ready to take her back. She pleaded with him for his forgiveness. She sent him letters, cards, gifts, and flowers. She called and spoke with Ted's frat brothers to appeal to him on her behalf. She even went to dinner with a couple of them but refused to go to bed with them, unless they can deliver Ted to her on a platter . . .

Some of Ted's frat brothers advised him to stay away from the Satan, Pat. They knew she was trouble. They knew she was evil. A few of Ted's advisors were still pissed off at her since she wouldn't give up her booty.

On one occasion, she had a one night stand with Ted in an all-expense paid trip by her, or maybe paid from her office expense account, to Las Vegas, to plead her case and asked for his forgiveness. She wanted to marry him at one of the sprawling chapels on the strip, ignoring the fact that Ted was already married. Her own marriage didn't count or matter. "What happens in Vegas stays in Vegas," she reminded him. Instead, Ted refused and flew back home the following morning because he couldn't perform nor wanted any part of the whole affair. The past rape accusation continued to hunt him psychologically, physically, and emotionally. He loved his wife too. The voice of his mother continued to warn him about the devil in sheep's clothing: Pat.

Ted had told her, before he departed, "Boobsy, I never stop loving you but let me be, and give me the chance to love my family. Do the same and love your husband. You forever hurt me. I'm trying to forgive but can't forget."

As fate would have it, Sheila had also dashed Pat's last hope to be with Ted by getting pregnant with her second child, Judas Augustus Samson. The rumor was that the cute boy favors Pat.

Consequently thereafter, Ted had ignored her presence by all means possible like the plague. He had refused to open or read her love letters, gifts, and e-mails. All her letters were returned unopened with the comment: return to sender, addressee doesn't live here anymore. Her gifts were donated to area charities—Goodwill Industries got most of them. Subsequently, he closed his Facebook and Tweeter accounts because of her constant posting and twits. He had considered moving out of town several times with his family, he only stayed for the benefit of his children's excellent school district and to obey his wife's wishes.

Pat subsequently appealed to Ted to allow her to be his mistress. She was willing to have his children without his involvement in their lives—she was willing to sign a contract to that effect. She was willing to leave her husband, Paul, for him, anytime he wanted. "Just name the time and I will be ready for you wherever you want me to be," she had written to him many times. She sent him numerous nude pictures of her best in the morning after shower, and before going to bet at night—one of her nude poses was similar to the statute of the Roman goddess during Emperor Augustus' reign.

Ted's answer was to avoid and ignore her, even when he knew he will forever be in love with her. To both, it was a tale of the same city . . .

Finally, she can now confess the ultimate truth in the present of her Lord, even though; her Lord Almighty already knew the truth, before she concocted her destructive plan to nail Ted's coffin:

Pat was the one who anonymously called Theodore Samson, on the night of February 5th, the night of her pre-arranged wedding anniversary celebration. She was the one who excused herself from her quest, Sheila, walked to her private bathroom, and called Ted at exactly 6:56pm, to inform him that his wife, Sheila, was at the residence of the acting chief of police as she speaks.

Her scolding telephone conversation with him, while disguising her voice, was harsh, mean, diabolical, and direct:

"Good evening Sam."

"Who this," Ted answered.

"Are you sitting down?"

"Who's speaking, please?" Ted cordially responded this time around.

"Why don't you sit down, shut the fuck up, and listen."

I just want to update you who your so-called wife has been fucking lately. Today is your lucky day, boy, if you learn to shut up your big mouth and . . .

"I think you got the wrong number, whoever you are," Ted said, and hung up. He sat down and was in a daze because he knew the caller was accurate about his wife. Who knew? How many people knew? Was it from one of her scorned girlfriends? Is blackmail in the works? Could it be Shamika, Sheila's boo of the month, harassing me because I kicked her out for practically living here? These and many more questions were running through his head.

Pat immediately called him back, this time, on his private cell phone. As soon as Ted picked up his iPhone7X, she said, "I got the right number Sammy. Your name is Theodore Samson, you live on . . . , and your stupid wife, Sheila, calls you Sammy. You have two children. Your daughter is studying classical needle work history of medieval period, and not doing so well at her Ivy League, you paid $51,487.15 a year, for the last two years . . . do you still want me to go on, or you want to listen, because ain't got all day for your sorry ass."

"Are you still there, Sammy boy?"

Ted, in a dejected manner answered, "Yes, I'm still here." He is now wondering how the caller got his private cell number and who the caller might be. He couldn't make out the distorted voice . . .

Remember the weekend you went to your best friend's funeral in Toledo and you called your slutty wife many times without an answer? And when she finally answered, she said she was sleeping over at her mom's and you asked why then should your son be spending the same night at his friend's house? She was sleeping alright, not with her mother, I promise you that much, Sammy boy. Remember on Halloween night, when a lady in Halloween clown-costume with gold mask was chatting with you; and your sorry ass wife offered you a drink, and your stupid idiot slept all night on the floor? She spiced your drink fool. By the way, it seems you'll have a promising career as a chef or butler, in case you change career in the future. I'm sure the names Milk and Sugar ring a bell. Got it now, moron?

Even when the whole world laughed in your face, you are too blind to see it. I know about all the dirty shit taking place in your household, as you pretend the entire world wouldn't notice. You are so stupid, stupid, stupid, and an idiot, because the whole world knew. I knew. We all knew. You are a weak man without a spine . . . By the way; I have pictures and tapes to support these claims. Maybe, I would post them on my Facebook and Flickr in due time if you don't believe me. I'll send you the links when I'm ready to post them. The social network community would've a field day about your stinking ass and your rotten image. Better yet, maybe I should send the pictures to that British based newspaper under investigations by the British parliament—they prey on such information, and I'm sure they would love it. Maybe, I would keep the dollars within our country, and send them to the tabloid in west coast—you have a copy of the trashy tabloid on your coffee table, last week. How far am I doing, mother-fucker?

Ted hung up his phone because he had had enough. Pat immediately called back but could only leave the rest of her scornful messages on his voice mail and said, "You can't hide fool."

If you hurry this evening, you might catch your wife fucking the acting chief of police by the pool with her husband watching . . . The entire town has been laughing behind your back about your wife fucking a top politician in town. They had made love in your bed, on your dining room table, on the loveseat in front of your fire place, and on two occasions, had slept together overnight in your daughter's room like the rest of her lesbian whores. After I hang up this phone, go to her second drawer in her closet, and you will find a sample of the evidence we have in our possession. They are wrapped underneath her leather jacket you bought for her three weeks ago for getting rid of the bitch you didn't like. You will love them, Buster . . . Sammy, what's wrong with you? It seems you can't handle more than one woman at any time.

You are so fucked, stupid fool.

Abruptly, Pat hung up and walked back to their quest, Queen Sheila, to continue their wedding day celebration. She was proud of her performances.

She wanted a revenge for Ted's rejection. She wanted to end his life, without a single bullet, because he had contributed to her unhappiness. She wanted to show him she has the ultimate control over his happiness, and was ready to destroy it at will. She wanted to remind him that he can run but cannot hide.

She wanted to show him the extent of a woman's scorn, rational or not, because she couldn't have him. "If I couldn't have him, no one should or would," she emphatically said aloud many times. She was a woman many will conclude has no conscience. Strangely though, she has a conscience; she just didn't give a damn. "Life meant nothing to me, no more," she told herself by the time plan C was put into action.

She wanted to blame him for his inability to read her mind with all they had shared together for the four years they loved each other unconditionally. In fact, she blamed him for all her problems to-date.

She had now achieved her mission, and in the process destroyed many lives, including Paul's. She had aided and abetted Paul's affairs with Sheila without his knowledge. She had planned Paul's demise which ultimately led to his suicide without regrets, days after she met Sheila in her Mansion in OldPort with her husband. She knew about Paul and Sheila's phone exchanges. She had all the tapes—over sixty hours long. She knew about Paul's every Wednesday visits to Sheila's and all her panties he took along with him. She had viewed Paul's sex tape with Sheila on digital, a few times live. After all, she had used the same technology to tape Sheila and her girls, at the same domicile, before Ted was forced to move out . . . She had used her police officers to spy on Paul many times. That was how the select committee, responsible to appoint a new chief of police, for the city of Kope, got wind of her nasty family affairs and passed her over for the position . . .

She blamed Ted when he visited her after the funeral service and then walked away from her again. She wished he had stayed for the night, held her close, and said, "Boobsy, we will be alright now. Make love to me, for the first time." In the end, Ted has become emotionally, physically, and physiologically useless to himself and anyone else. Finally, she had overplayed her hands.

On this solemn day, at this lonely time in her life, Pat finally accepted the fact that she had set the platform of self-destruction, by her own agenda, without an exit strategy. She knew she had sinned. She was too guilty to ask her God for forgiveness at her evening prayers.

She started crying and shaking uncontrollably. She was alone now in the entire world. She was pacing around contemplating her next line of action. She has no more tangible options. To her, life is meaningless. To her, life had become a blur. She had embarked on revenge, and by so doing, dug one big hole for Ted. Unfortunately, the hole was spacious enough for her and Ted.

———————————————————•●•——————————————————

She wanted to do everything within her power to look for Sheila and begged for her forgiveness. She wanted to be on her knees and said to her, "Sheila, all will be fine. We will raise Paul's son together. We have the means, the strength, and the love for each other to sustain any obstacles."

She wanted to look for her and say, "Sheila, come home and let us create our own happiness as it was meant to be. I'm all yours now, Sheila. I'm all yours. Today, I too will finally confess that I love you. I want us to be together for the rest of our lives. Paul is out of our lives now. Ted is no longer significant as well." She never thought she will fall madly in love with the lady she planned to destroy in other to have her husband . . .

In the final analysis, Pat, the lady who wanted everything
her way, the woman who had been troubled and unsuitable in
the world in which she created, and the woman who, for all
practical purposes a control freak, had now joined the legions
of men and women of the universe, blinded by their own
ambition and greed.

The Lord created the gang of four so perfectly. The Lord
also gave them everlasting life and power over all things
under the sun, and by Pat's actions, with the support of her
main conspirator, Sheila, she destroyed all that was good and
decent in her life and the lives of others around her. What a
pity. What a waste of God's perfect creation.

She took a deep breath and swallowed a big gulp of her
Bacardi rum concoction, and drifted off to sleep from mental
exhaustion. She fell asleep but still not at peace.

In her dream, she saw three Angels circling over her bed,
touching wings, as they joined hands trying to pray for the
redemption of her soul. Her mother and her husband, Paul,
were two of the angels. Her mother had passed away six
months prior to Paul's death.

In unison, the angels asked Jesus Christ, on her behalf,
"Lord, teach us one more time, how to pray for this sinner."

Sheila sat at the edge of her bed, closed her eyes, and joined
the angels in reciting the Lord's Prayer:

> *Our Father, which art in heaven,*
> *Hallowed be thy name. Thy Kingdom come*
> *Thy will be done in earth,*
> *as it is in heaven.*
> *Give us this day our daily bread.*
> *And forgive us our trespasses,*

as we forgive those that trespass against us.
And lead us not into temptation,
but deliver us from evil.
For thine are the kingdom, the power, and the glory,
orever and ever.
Amen.

"Thank you Lord, her body and soul are in your hands now," the angels said.

As the angels were ascending into the heavens, they said unto her: "Patricia, you're cleansed and all your sins are forgiven for the last time. Go in perfect peace and sin no more."

She went back to bed peacefully. This time, she was at peace for the first time in weeks.

CHAPTER 24

Minutes later, Pat was finally awakened for breakfast, by a flight attendant, aboard Amabo International Airlines, cruising at 39,000 feet over the Atlantic for the last fifteen hours.

She looked around, perplexed, dazed, confused, and realized that she was on her way back from the Holy Land on a religious/family vacation.

Sitting on her left, holding her hand tightly, was Sheila Maureen Samson. Sitting on Sheila's left was attorney Theodore Samson, IV, leaning against the window smiling while watching the onboard movie, Family Affairs.

Sheila looked at Pat's pale and troubled face and asked, "Pat, are you ok? You're sweating bullets."

Pat said aside, "Sweet Jesus, it was all a dream. I've been dreaming everything all along. Thank you Jesus."

"What did you say?" Sheila asked.

"Never mind, sis," I'm ok.

She asked for a glass of water and a warm wet towel from the flight attendant.

———————————•●•———————————

The sad truth, however, was that her dream was a combination of fantasies and realities.

The realities of her current circumstances which must finally be told are these:

Pat's true name is Pamela Harrison, the daughter of Helen Peterman-Harrison. She is a beautiful 31-year old mother of twin boys she had while a freshman in college. Unable to cope with her studies, children, and social obligations, she dropped out of school to raise her children and get her life back on tract. Ten years later, she was able to obtain an associate certificate in dental/nursing online, from one of the for-profit cyber community colleges.

At the age of thirty, she married a twenty-three year old marine Sargent, Michael. She wanted a man with dependable job who can also be a father figure for her boys. Michael was such a man. He was her type and willing to play any roles she demanded of him. They had met at one of her friend's bachelorette party. Michael was one of the strippers at the joyous event.

Since the age of fourteen, she has been working at the law firm of Theodore Samson & Associates, PLLC. At twenty nine, with her associate certificate, she was promoted as the executive personal assistant to the fifty-eight year old founder of the law firm, attorney Samson, IV. He once represented her in her child support and alimony lawsuit against the father of her twin boys. Unfortunately, her "Baby-daddy" is still unemployed and living with his mama without the means to pay the judgments against him. She refused to send him to jail. Frankly, he's still a pothead at the age of thirty-eight.

Attorney Theodore Samson's financial support and understanding during her many ordeals attracted him to her. She went out with him a couple of times. He became her mentor, confidant, and the center of her universe—practically her savior and redeemer for everything she wanted under the sun. After a couple of dates, she called him, Teddy. He called her, Iris. The dates were innocent at first, and Teddy's fatherly role in her life mesmerized her. Most importantly, he was financially loaded as a trial lawyer and a timeshare developer, before the housing bubble.

She was the one that had a threesome with him and his cousin in one of the year-end get away office parties in Cancun. She always blamed that episode on alcohol, drug experimentation, loneliness, undue influence, and office politics. In reality, she wanted to be closer to her Teddy, and at the same time, consolidate the power of her new office as his executive personal secretary, with a corner office. She spent most of her valuable time, marking and protecting her little official kingdom.

In addition, for the past five months, she had been sleeping regularly with him when in need. She was always in need, financially and otherwise. She was the one that demanded a brand new car from him as an incentive to keep her mouth shut about their sexual rendezvous from her family. She was the one who sent a bouquet of flowers to his house to thank him for the new car on their one year anniversary, and to celebrate the first time they made love at the back of his gold Suburban—made in USA. He was the one who sent her the ceased-desist letter from his lawyer because his wife was having issues with more than usual flowers from unknown clients . . .

His excuses, "The flowers were from satisfied clients," was no longer convincing to his wife who always suspected he was fucking around. After all, his wife seduced him when he was representing her during her second divorce. He was married at the time—it seems money and gorgeous women go hand in hand, in the secluded club of trial lawyers . . .

For the most part, Pat's excuses for going after Teddy were simple, "Attorney Samson's dick is too good to ignore and his generosity can't be surpassed. "He's mine and no one else should have him. He's fine, healthy for his age, and a generous man who knows how to use his rod extraordinarily." That was how she justified her twisted soul each time she felt guilty and realized the destructive consequences of her reckless association and endeavors. Like most children of God, she never thought about the resolve of her actions or whose life she might destroy in the process.

A pregnancy test has just confirmed that she is forty two days pregnant by her employer/lover/father-figure, attorney Theodore Samson, IV.

In her dream, Paul committed suicide at the age of forty two.

To make matters worse, attorney Theodore Samson, IV, is her twin sister's husband of two years and six weeks. He had no children with her sister, Sheila Maureen Samson, a.k.a, Disaya, who already had five brats of her own from two previous marriages. The sixth child was as a result of one night-stand. The one night-stand gentleman, who was only known to her, to this day, as Snake L, had disappeared since the night of their hot sexual encounter. His last sighting was somewhere in the great state of Taxes. Disaya was certain; she wouldn't recognize him even if he is in a one-man police line-up. She had secretly performed tubal ligation after her last child, without disclosing the fact to her husband, Samson, who always wanted a son to carry on his legacy. He never adopted Disaya's children.

In less than three days, Pat's husband, Sargent Michael, will be coming home after six months' deployment in Afghanistan.

There was one problem: Pamela (Pat) can't confront her husband, her mother, her twin sister, and attorney Samson, about her current dilemma. "How on earth do I get pregnant when we always use condoms," she lamented. She forgot the birthday celebration with Teddy and his cousin on February 5th, when Teddy didn't use condoms. What's more, she couldn't justify why she went too far and did what she did to her own loving sister. Her twin sister had been her best friend and a supporter when everyone else abandoned her. She has no rational reason for her selfish actions except that she is a loose girl with insatiable sex addiction, and not her soro sister, as she dreamt it. She did what she did to her real sister.

What an irony:

She was the one expecting a child for her sister's husband. She was the one cheating on her marine husband while serving his country overseas. She was the one who had a threesome with Teddy and his cousin on February 5th. She was the one fucked by Teddy's cousin doggy style with condom.

She was the one playing with the possibility of losing her husband due to her sexual addiction, regardless of whom she destroyed in the process. She was the one who refused to open her door for her mother when she visited her apartment unannounced—her mother knocked endlessly, on one or two occasions, when Teddy was at her house for dinner and much more . . .

She was the one that told Teddy that she is ready to remain his mistress, and willing to keep her mouth shut, as long as he provides for her and her children—she got a brand new car as part of the agreement. She was the one that kept video tapes of her encounters with Teddy, in case he reneges on their verbal agreements. She also kept audio tapes of all verbal agreements with her other personal junk, in her mother's house. She was the one that placed a copy of one of their sex tapes on Ted's desk to remind him of his responsibility and obligations, when he refused to pay her monthly maintenance allowance on schedule. She had refused to spend one more night a week with him in the company-owned condo, overlooking the Bay—Teddy simply wanted more mileage for his money. A woman with her assets shouldn't blame any man for wanting more—the Oliver Twist's type of men. Again, there seem to be Oliver in every man. Correction: there is Oliver in almost every man and woman . . .

She was the one who lied to her husband when he called from undisclosed location in Afghanistan, while entertaining Teddy, countless times, to say that she was having dinner with her mother, Sheila, and her children.

Pamela did the Arithmetic, it didn't add up. Her hope might not be lost, however. There is a slim chance, in her whopped mind that the unborn child might belong to Teddy's cousin. She knew being fucked with a condom is twelve percent unreliable. Now, she prayed for the twelve percent. Unfortunately, her memory was still playing game with her sick mind—she forgot that Teddy's cousin fucked her only in her asshole with condom. Clearly, Pat and her secret father-figure-lover are truly fucked, so to speak.

There was one last crucial fact, attorney Theodore Samson, IV, is a damned good trial lawyer with plenty of money, connections, and capable of pulling a rabbit out of a hat.

Better yet, Pat has one last alternative or maybe two. One of her alternatives is not an option for attorney Samson, period. He already knew she was pregnant.

It's amazing how dreams sometimes parallel real life, some of the time.

I hope y'all held your judgment. I had held mine . . .